the
possibility
of

fireflies

by
dominique paul

simon & schuster books for young readers
new york   london   toronto   sydney

SIMON & SCHUSTER BOOKS FOR YOUNG READERS
An imprint of Simon & Schuster Children's Publishing Division
1230 Avenue of the Americas, New York, New York 10020
This book is a work of fiction. Any references to historical events, real people, or real locales are used fictitiously. Other names, characters, places, and incidents are the product of the author's imagination, and any resemblance to actual events or locales or persons, living or dead, is entirely coincidental.
Copyright © 2006 by Dominique Paul
SIMON & SCHUSTER BOOKS FOR YOUNG READERS is a trademark of Simon & Schuster, Inc.
Book design by Lizzy Bromley
The text of this book was set in Life.
Manufactured in the United States of America
10 9 8 7 6 5 4 3 2 1
Library of Congress Cataloging-in-Publication Data
Paul, Dominique.
The possibility of fireflies / by Dominique Paul.— 1st S&S ed.
p. cm.
Summary: Fourteen-year-old Ellie fights to keep her life together while her emotionally unstable mother deteriorates and her rebellious older sister begins to hang out with a rough crowd.
ISBN-13: 978-1-4169-1310-8
ISBN-10: 1-4169-1310-6
[1. Mothers and daughters—Fiction. 2. Family problems—Fiction. 3. Sisters—Fiction.]
I. Title.
PZ7.P278343Po 2006
[Fic]—dc22
2005029903

FIRST
EDITION

for
cammy

There is an inmost center in us all,
Where truth abides in fullness; . . . and, to know,
Rather consists in opening out a way
Whence the imprisoned splendor may escape,
Than in effecting entry for a light
Supposed to be without.

—from "Paracelsus,"
by Robert Browning

one

I am sitting on my front stoop. The rows of townhouses, some of them brick, some that colorful metal stuff, face me in the dark. I think it's about midnight. I was busy reading up until an hour ago, but my eyes started to hurt from squinting. Now it's just me and the waiting.

I'm getting good at this. My mother does this lately . . . leaves me out here. She says she forgets. She goes out a lot these days and sometimes she forgets to leave a key for me. She says I can't be trusted with my own set of keys, so my older sister Gwen and I devised a plan. We unlatch the back window in case this happens, then we can crawl through and just go on to bed. But I checked, and the window is locked too. Gwen must be at a friend's house for the night. A *school* night. Can you imagine?

I had gone to a friend's house after school, but her dad dropped me off here at eight o'clock. Sometimes I go home on the bus with my best friend, Celia, even though Celia says it is beneath us to ride the school bus because we are in the ninth grade now. The school bus doesn't go all the way to my house. It stops at the end of Turkey Foot Road and then I have to walk two miles, which never seems like a good idea to me.

I love going to Celia's house, bus or no bus. Her mom, Mrs. Meyers, waits for us at the top of the driveway. She used to wait at the bottom of the drive, but then Celia reminded her that we are almost fifteen, so now she waits at the top. Mrs. Meyers is a natural redhead with watery blue eyes and a cherubic smile. She usually smells like Pine-Sol and she always kisses *both* of us, leaving perfect pink lip marks on our faces. She always asks specific questions about our day. Like for instance today she asked me, "Ellie honey"—she says that like it's one word—"what happened with your idea for your Shakespeare class?" and I skipped alongside her into the kitchen because I knew she was wondering if my English teacher agreed that it was a good idea to have the kids read all the parts aloud like Shakespeare himself intended. So when she asked me this, I was able to report back that, indeed, we would now be reading aloud with the parts preassigned so we could practice.

"Well," Mrs. Meyers said enthusiastically, "that'll be just like a play every day in fourth period."

That was my favorite part. I said it over and over in my head, *a play every day,* and pictured myself standing in front of the class reciting the prose of poor, wounded Ophelia.

She served Celia and me lemon bars and milk at the kitchen table, where we looked through *Star Hits* magazine at pictures of all the latest Brit Pop cuties, Duran Duran being our favorite. Celia and I both think John Taylor is the cutest, and sometimes it is the source of some tension between us. We are both afraid that John will like the other more. Celia for her long legs, me for my hair. Celia says the way my hair feathers all the way down the sides and meets in the back is enviable. But I still say that is second to being leggy. I try to sell her on Simon's good points (he's a *poet,* I tell her), but so far she's not buying it.

After we ate our snack and were done with the *Star Hits,* we went up to her room to do our homework. Celia's room is a shrine to Duran Duran. Every inch of her walls is covered; she even cut out small pictures of the band from newspapers to cover the molding on her bedroom door.

At six thirty we heard her dad come home from work. Mrs. Meyers didn't greet him outside because she was busy making dinner, which is always at six forty-five. We went downstairs and headed for the kitchen.

"Hi, Daddy." Celia kissed her dad on his cheek. "Mom? Ellie's gonna stay for dinner, 'kay?"

"Sure. If it's okay with her mother."

That was the fun part because—and I do this every time—I walked over to the phone *feigning dread* in an effort to appear as though I wasn't sure *what* my mother would say. Could I stay? Would my presence be demanded at home at once? What, oh what, would the outcome be? The whole evening hung in the balance.

Then I picked up the phone and dialed the time.

Of course, my mother was well on her way to happy hour at

that point. But I proceeded, as usual, to have a lengthy conversation for the benefit of everyone in the room. I nervously asked the automated clock if it would be okay for me to stay at the Meyerses' for dinner. One time when I did this I got carried away and said, "Oh, you were going to make coq au vin?" I don't even know what that is, but, boy, does it sound good. "Could we save it for tomorrow?" I'm careful not to do that anymore, though, because Mrs. Meyers began gesturing wildly from across the room in a manner that could only mean, "Oh no, no, dear, if your mom is going to all that trouble . . . ," and I had to quickly hang up. God forbid she might ask to speak to my mother! She'd grab the receiver from me with her usual zeal only to hear, "At the tone the time will be . . ." The horror.

I hung up the phone. "She says it's fine." Celia winked at me, knowing.

Tonight Mrs. Meyers made pasta primavera. All I can say is, *Wow.* Penne pasta with a myriad of fresh vegetables she cut herself: broccoli, peppers, carrots, zucchini—too many to count. Plus a salad with walnuts in it, plus bread. Rosemary bread with a very hard but yummy crust. Even dessert. Did I mention it's only Tuesday? Strawberries over angel cake with Cool Whip.

Celia's parents had wine with dinner, and Mrs. Meyers asked if it would be okay with my mother if I had a little wine with them.

Sometimes adults do this; they try to include you in a way that is well-intentioned if not entirely appropriate. But when this sort of thing happens, I have a ready response. "Oh, it's fine. I'm Italian, it's normal." And that is true. I *am* Italian. My dad is full-blooded Italian and my mom is mostly Italian and a little Irish, too.

Mr. Meyers, who hardly ever speaks, said that I didn't look Italian, and I said that I was fair like my mom and my sister was dark like my dad. This explanation always seems to satisfy everyone. Like if at least some of us have dark skin and hair, then we are authentic Italians. My sister has the dark skin and hair, but her eyes are green just like mine. Of course, they are a lot more striking on her. Green eyes with dishwater-blond hair and fair skin just don't have the same effect as they do when everything else is dark. Trust me on this. Relatives, strangers, everyone on the street says to Gwen, "What beautiful eyes you have!" I feel like waving a banner that says, "Hel-*lo*! Mine are the *exact* same color!"

"How's your mom liking her new job?" asked Mr. Meyers.

"She likes it," I told him. "She says to say thank you."

"It was my pleasure."

Celia's dad is a doctor. A few months ago, when my mom lost her job at the insurance company, he got her a job with a friend of his who deals in medical supplies. She's the office manager. My mom can type sixty words per minute, plus she knows shorthand.

I filled up on pasta and salad, *and* bread, *and* dessert. I even had a few sips of red wine, which wasn't very good, not that I'm complaining. You probably think I'm not old enough to know the good stuff from the rest when it comes to wine, but this is not true. A by-product of growing up Italian is that you know a lot about wine. My dad always says, "Life is too short to drink bad wine." When I was growing up, he would spend more than we had on nice bottles of wine for special occasions like Christmas. This would infuriate my mother, and she would yell things like who did he think he was, buying wine like that, and didn't he know he was just a steelworker's son from Pennsylvania no matter what his degrees said. They fought a lot, my parents. Then finally, about a year ago, my dad left.

After dinner, Celia and I did homework, and then Mr. Meyers drove me home. When we pulled into my neighborhood and neared the corner to our townhouse, I could see that no lights were on.

Seeing the concerned look on his face, I told Mr. Meyers our porch light was broken. "My mom's been meaning to get that fixed," I lied.

I grabbed my backpack and climbed out of the truck. They just bought a teal green Suzuki Samurai. Celia says it will be hers when she turns sixteen.

"Thanks for the ride. Good night," I called over my shoulder as I slowly made my way to the front door.

"Good night!" I said again and waved really big as though to say, *You can go now.* But he didn't drive off.

"I'll just watch you go on in," he said sleepily and adjusted his glasses on his face.

Shit. Now what? I casually lifted the welcome mat with my foot (the irony here was not lost on me) and looked down for a key. Nothing. I needed a plan.

"I'll just go around back and get my dog," I said.

Oh, great, like *that* was believable. We don't even have a dog anymore. But this was my plan: I figured I'd sneak in through the back window, unlock the front door, go back out the back door, walk around front, and just go in the door like a normal person. Truth be told, I just wasn't ready for the Meyerses or anyone else to know that no one was home; that it seemed like no one was ever home; that I am fourteen and regularly locked out of my own house because my mother has decided, and I quote, "to take a vacation from parenting." What would they think of me?

I walked to the back of the house and checked the window. Locked. Either Gwen was a total dip or Mom found it unlocked. You'd think it was Fort Knox in there, the way she is about the locks. I considered this for a moment and resolved that I would just have to lie.

I marched around to the front and announced, "My sister has taken the dog for a walk. It is such a nice night; I just love this time of year . . . I think I'll just sit outside and watch the fireflies while I wait for her." I said this with as much conviction as I could muster and held my breath as Mr. Meyers considered it.

"Are you sure?" Mr. Meyers hesitated. Oh, yes, I said. Completely sure. Go on home. I'll be fine. Then he drove off and left me in the dark as I'd insisted.

It was a lie, of course. But these days lies seem to slip off my tongue more easily than the truth. The lies just sound better, more palatable. I mean, I couldn't very well say my mother was out God knows where, doing God knows what, and had locked me out again, could I? Besides, our neighbor's mom knows the truth, and now Jennie's not allowed to talk to me anymore. She walks right by me at school and acts like she doesn't know who I am. So instead I said that I am restless and want to enjoy the night, want to watch the fireflies as they light up like stars right in front of me. Now, isn't that better? And if you think about it, isn't it just a little true? I realize that the truth is becoming malleable for me, this thing I can shape and manipulate to suit me. Granted, I'm just trying to survive here, but one day this could be a big problem. Don't sociopaths and murderers do the very same thing? Maybe it's better just to tell people what is really going on, to reveal the truth no matter how hard it is to swallow. But first, I suppose I would have to understand what is really going on, and that is a whole thing unto itself.

All I can say is, since my dad left, my mother has . . . not so much *changed* . . . it's more like she's come unraveled. Like he was the last bit of glue that was keeping her together, and now that he's gone, all the broken parts can take over. I haven't quite figured it out yet. All I know is, it feels like nothing makes sense anymore. And there are days, like today, when the world seems very far away.

It's still too early in the year for honeysuckle, so instead I inhale the smell of the first mown grass in bags. Equally pleasurable. I can picture the sweaty husbands mowing all day while their wives bring them ice-cold sun tea and mop their brows. I've always wanted to make sun tea. You have to use like twenty tea bags or something. My mom likes the instant, powdered kind. I think it's too sweet, and one time when I said so, she told me I should get a job and buy my own then. Sometimes you just never know where it's gonna come from with her. A simple thing like tea.

My eyelids are so heavy I can't fight it anymore. The fireflies are tired too now and have stopped using their lights, though I suspect they are still out there flying silently in the dark, hovering in the distance like silent guardians. I snuggle into my backpack and am about to fold into sleep when the knowledge spoons up behind me and rests its head on my shoulder: Apart from the possibility of fireflies, I am alone. It is just me and darkness . . . and hope.

two

IF there is one thing I have to say, it is this: High school is completely overrated. Everyone keeps talking about it being the best years of your life, but so far I am not impressed. It is the middle of May and I am nearly at the end of my freshman year, and, quite frankly, the whole darn thing has stunk out loud. Here's the evidence:

1. I have no friends, save for Celia. In my defense, I feel I should point out that we relocated to Rockshire from Boonesville, a small town about thirty miles away, at the very end of last summer. This did not give me enough time to cultivate friendships with the kids in my neighborhood, and I had to start cold, whereas the other kids had all of elementary school and junior high, *plus* the summer. Add to that that my mother wasn't happy with the first house we moved into in Rockshire, so we moved into another neighborhood just as I was beginning to get my flow. Wait. It gets worse. Then she decided she didn't like that house either and we moved *again*. Next door. So any friends I could have made in my new neighborhood were cancelled out because we were labeled as freaks. You should have seen us. We didn't even box our stuff. We just carried it from one house to the next. When we got down to the big pieces of furniture, my mom paid the paperboy forty dollars to help us out.

2. Despite the fact that this is supposed to be the big city— and, admittedly, it *is* more entertaining than Boonesville— Rockshire hasn't got much going for it. Sure, there are movie theaters and malls, but mostly it's just another crappy suburb in Maryland on the outskirts of Baltimore. Everyone's parents either work for the government or for the school system. I've heard some kids at school talking about going out to Georgetown on weekends, but so far I am not on speaking terms with those kids. I'm still just that weird new girl from Boonesville, as far as they can tell. I keep wanting to pull out a map and show them that Boonesville is not that far away. You don't even have to turn off Route 90; you just keep going north and in about thirty minutes you are there. But just the way they say *Boones*ville makes me realize that to them it is a place so far away from their world that they don't even want to try to fathom it.

When I got to homeroom on the very first day of school, the teacher introduced all the new kids. I had to stand up and say where I was from and if I had any siblings and why we had moved to Rockshire. I got as far as, "My name is Ellie and I moved here from Boonesville," and I just heard their eyes rolling.

3. My schedule is from hell. I have gym first period! Aerobics. I wake up and shower at home because my mother makes me, only to go to school, change into my gym clothes, and sweat all over the place.

Our teacher, Mrs. Corvelli, is losing her hair, so she's not that comfortable jumping around in case her wig slides. She's not sick or anything, she just has a special condition. She's devised this system of letting some of the girls lead the class in our routines. We do the same Jane Fonda tape every day, so why we need a leader at this point is beyond me. It's volunteer only, so of course the same painfully perky three girls do it every time. Not all at once; Mrs. Corvelli lets them alternate. They look exactly the same and come with equally interchangeable names like Jodi and Jennifer. They all have the same long brown hair that is heavily frosted and permed, with the bangs so high and crispy they look like a claw on their foreheads. They wear tight leggings in various cheerful colors and matching sports bras, two pairs of color-coordinated socks each, finished off with brand-new white Reebok high-tops. Just picture me in the red sweatpants I've had since sixth-grade camp (before the growth spurt) that now almost come up to my shins, my dad's Pittsburgh Steelers T-shirt, *barefoot,* huffing and puffing at seven A.M., and you will know the hell that is my life.

I go from that indignity to yet another: Math. Algebra to be exact. I got a D last semester, not that anyone noticed. I tried explaining to my teacher, Mr. Shiner, that my brain just doesn't work that way. I'm not really a numbers kind of gal, I said. He wasn't too happy with that. He just kind of glared at me with a sweaty top lip. That kind of creeped me out, because it wasn't even hot in there. The other thing is that I just can't relate to formulas. I mean, when in real life does A plus B ever equal C? Nothing is ever that simple; there are all kinds of mitigating circumstances that throw it off. If there is one thing I know, it's that life is complicated, and when you are expecting a certain outcome, you'd better prepare for the other one just in case. My obvious conclusion is that Algebra is not based in truth and is irrelevant. But my teacher just thinks I'm some smart aleck–wisenheimer now. You should see Mr. Shiner. He weighs three hundred pounds and has really tiny feet.

After Math we have this thing called Flex. A fifteen-minute break between second and third period. This is the highlight of my morning so far, for this reason: The cafeteria sells chocolate-chip cookies. Not just any chocolate-chip cookies, either. Hot, soft ones bigger than your hand. And they only cost thirty cents. I can always scrounge up enough money for a cookie. Technically, it's my breakfast, so I'm not indulging in a forbidden treat or anything.

When I was growing up, my mom used to make us pancakes for breakfast. She used this big cast-iron skillet and she would make one huge pancake exactly the size of the pan. Gwen and I used to cut off squares of butter and put it on the pancake while it was still finishing in the skillet. Then we ate it right out of the pan, but eventually I had to ask if we could split it up onto plates because Gwen would always drown the darn thing in syrup. She has a heavy hand, that Gwen. Most often, though, my mom bought us those big-name cereals my friends' parents wouldn't let them eat. My favorite was Fruity Pebbles, and when I was all done with the cereal I'd drink the milk after it had turned a soothing shade of pink. Gwen liked Golden Grahams. But we don't have money for big brands like that anymore, and I can't tell you the last time my mother got out of bed in time for pancakes.

Third period is Government. Need I say more? I mean, I'm not even old enough to vote. *Sheez.*

Fourth period is English. I have a great teacher, Mr. Conway. He wears bow ties and rides his bicycle to school. He puts his papers and his lunch in the little basket nestled between the handlebars. There were rumors about Mr. Conway at the beginning of the year, but then we found out he was married. I couldn't care less about that; he's the best teacher I ever had, for several reasons. One, he doesn't play favorites. He calls on all the kids in class, not just the popular ones like my other teachers do. In his room, the caste system of high school does not exist. That is refreshing because, as you may or may not have guessed, I have a long way to go if I am to become popular.

Mostly, I think I like English best, because I don't have to study very hard for the spelling and vocabulary tests. The reason is because, if I read over the list a couple of times, it gets printed in my brain. I know it sounds sensational, but I mean it. I can read it right out of my head and copy it down during the test. I used to think it was kind of like cheating, but I can't help it from happening. Celia said it's called *photographic memory,* and she saw a thing on TV about it. She said it's a rare thing and she acted really weird to me that whole day, like we were different. I think she was just mad that I don't have to study as long as she does for vocab.

I also like the stuff we read in English class. Last month we read a play called *Our Town,* and oh, did I ever love it! In this play people come back from the dead to take a look back on one day of their lives. Relive it, so to speak. My favorite character, Emily, chose to relive her sixth birthday party. Wouldn't that be something? She stood by and watched her whole family, all those years ago, buzzing around in their little kitchen worrying about the details of the day. She saw her mom preparing the cake and her little six-year-old self fretting over which dress to wear and so forth. In the play, the dead Emily got upset because the time was going by so fast and everyone was so caught up in the details that they weren't even looking at one another. When Mr. Conway asked the class what we thought about Emily's reaction, I raised my hand and said that I understood what she meant, but maybe she could look at it another way. He nodded for me to go on, so I did, even though I heard the other kids shuffling in their seats. I said it's a pretty special thing to have people fuss over your birthday, and maybe when they're fussing like that, you just know you are loved and you don't have to stop and take note of it. Like, it's okay to take it for granted because you're a kid and kids should be allowed to do that. Mr. Conway liked my answer and he winked at me. After a pause he said, "Class, when you grow up and somebody loves you, make sure you *know* it. With all of your being!" I love Mr. Conway. He has such a flair for the dramatic.

Next is Biology. Dreadful. I am proud to say that last month I exercised my right to forego the fetal-pig dissection. I just couldn't bear it. I mean, when they brought those little piggies out and I saw them all pink and undone I thought I'd have a heart attack. Their little hoofs hadn't even formed yet. It's like some jerk just went in and said nope, you don't get a chance, we're not even going to let you *try*. All the boys in the class started horsing around and chasing the girls with them. I raised my hand right there and then and said to my teacher that I couldn't do it on account of it was against my morals. Everyone started laughing at me. My teacher, Mrs. Price, raised a dis-approving eyebrow, but I stuck to it. I said I couldn't go and tear those little creatures apart anymore than they already had been when someone tore them out of their mothers. I said how would you feel if someone just took *your* mama away like that. Then everyone really started laughing, because I'd said *mama*. When I get going, you can tell I grew up in Boonesville. Mrs. Price finally said okay and let me go sit in the faculty lounge until class was over. On our way down the hall to the lounge, she said she didn't realize I was a vegetarian. I said neither did I. It's funny how sometimes you just know in your gut when a thing is wrong and when you can get away with saying so.

U.S. History comes next. I have to admit that sometimes it is kind of interesting. I think I might actually enjoy the class if Mr. Finkle weren't always trying to guilt us all to death. It's like he can't just say that George Washington was a good man, he has to always add how grateful we should be that our fore-fathers broke their backs for us like they did. Not to be mean, but nobody *made* them do anything. I had to reach this conclusion out of necessity. When we studied English colonization, I thought I would burst from all the residual guilt. I felt so bad for all those countries, and then for our own country and how horrible we were to the Indians. When I thought I would die from the shame I came up with this rationalization: My fore-fathers are Italian, so surely they were not involved in all this tyranny. I wrote this on a note and passed it to Celia. She wrote back: *Hey, Mr. Finkle, stick that in your guilt pipe and smoke it!* We started cracking up so hard we had to lay our heads on our desks so he couldn't see. Sometimes we get separated, Celia and me.

My last period of the day is Study Hall, and it is only bearable because of my only other friend in school, Greg. He's older than me, sixteen, and he *drives*. He is very tall, like six foot three, and he has dark hair, but he's not what you'd describe as tall-dark-and-handsome. I'm not one to criticize, so let's just say that Greg has yet to grow into his looks. All of his features seem way too big for his face. He told me he'd had a rather sudden growth spurt last year, so I don't think he's used to taking up all that extra headroom yet. Plus, I don't think his mom has had a chance to take him shopping, because he's still wearing his pre-growth-spurt clothes. All his shirts and pants are just a little too short and a little too tight. When he wears his black jeans, I get really uncomfortable for him.

We spend most of the period passing notes instead of doing

homework, which is the whole point of Study Hall. The best thing is that I can usually count on him to give me a ride home. I think he started doing it because he's hot for Gwen. Everyone's hot for Gwen. At first, when he would drop me off, he'd ask me if he could come inside and see her room. But he doesn't do that anymore. He is officially my friend now.

His mom lets him drive her Honda Accord to school, and I swear it is the cleanest car I have ever seen. It's six years old and still smells brand-new. When we climbed into the car today after class I finally asked Greg how this was possible. He said it was a special air freshener he asks them to use at the car wash.

"What's it called?" I asked.

"The car freshener?"

"Yeah."

"New Car," he said matter-of-factly.

"New Car? They actually have a freshener called New Car?"

"New Car *Smell,* actually," he corrected himself.

"So people just say 'Gimme that New Car Smell!' and they can get it?"

"*Yes,*" he said, getting exasperated. "Why is that so amazing to you?"

"It just seems so . . ."

"So *what*?"

"So . . . *easy,*" I said finally.

"Yeah," he said. "I guess it is." Then, "Some things are just easy to get."

"I guess you just gotta know you can ask."

He looked at me with a mixture of curiosity and wonder. That was the best part of all. Me, amazing someone like that.

Today when we got to my street I asked Greg if he would keep driving. He sped up past the turn, past the neighborhood sign, and we disappeared over the hill, no questions asked. I settled into my seat and tightened my seat belt around me. I couldn't go in there yet. My outsides felt like a softshell crab, still covering me but penetrable. I'd have to stay out a while longer, till they got good and hard again.

three

on some level, of course, I understand that change is normal. Necessary, even. But for the record I would just like to say the following to the disembodied entity that has taken over my sister Gwen's body: *Get out! Find a new body to squat in! I want my sister back! You're making me nuts!*

Or something to that effect.

I in no way mean to imply that things between Gwen and me were always copacetic, preentity. I assure you, we had our differences. But for the most part she was my pal. In fact, we shared a room up until last year. When my mom started talking about moving again, she said it was because Gwen and I were getting older and needed our own rooms. She used it as part of her sales pitch, not like our opinion was going to change her mind, anyway. And deep down I'd have to admit I was relieved about that, because Gwen had begun listening to heavy metal, the really hard stuff, too, like Slayer and Iron Maiden, and some of the posters she was putting up on the walls were giving me nightmares.

However, there are places where our musical tastes coincide, or at least I pretend they do. For example, right now we are sitting on the couch watching David Letterman. Jon Bon Jovi and Richie Sambora are scheduled to perform a special acoustic set of their song "Wanted Dead or Alive" tonight. Gwen didn't want to miss it; she just loves Richie Sambora. She used to be hot for Vince Neil, but now it is *all* about Richie. I agree with her that Richie is cute, but diplomatically say I like Jon better, so as not to run into the same problems I have with Celia about John Taylor. It's best not to overstep on this kind of stuff. Truthfully, though, I don't really care either way. I mean, I like the song, but I think he's hitting it a little too on the nose with the metaphors. It's like: *Rocker equals cowboy, get it?* Uh, yeah, I think we got it.

Suddenly there is a hard tapping on the window. I nearly jump out of my skin, but Gwen moves right over and opens it up.

"How do you know it's not a murderer?" I say.

"Oh, *please*. Don't be such a baby."

When she opens the window and I see that it's Justina Simpson, I know I'd better act cool or they are gonna kick me right out of here, and then I'll be up in my room missing everything.

Justina Simpson is Gwen's new best friend. Next to Justina, I am mammoth. She stands five feet nothing, a perfect size zero. I doubt her weight is in the triple digits. She has enviable long, blond hair that perfectly feathers all the way down the sides. Her uniform is always some variation of the following: heavy-metal-concert T-shirt, tight designer jeans, and Converse hightops, also known as Chucks. She has Chucks in every color, and sometimes she wears like one purple one and one green one.

Justina crawls through the window; she is so tiny, she fits easily. Immediately, I can tell she is stressed, because she is not her usual slow-moving self. Usually she is way too cool to rush. If there is a car waiting for her to cross an intersection, she will purposely slow down to an elderly pace and give the impatient driver a triumphant glare.

Gwen and I watch her pace back and forth across the living room; it's like watching a tennis match. I can tell she's been crying even though she didn't want us to see, but her black eye makeup is running down her face and she keeps chasing it back up to her eye with her shirtsleeve.

"Man," she snorts. "My mom is so lame. Fuck her, man."

Gwen shifts into cool mode, as I do around Justina. Always the empathizer, Gwen keeps telling her, "Walk it off, dude, just walk it off."

I decide to remain quiet in case they've only forgotten I'm here, instead of letting me stay, which is what I hope is happening.

Justina continues to pace back and forth, pausing now and then to turn to us for dramatic effect. Finally, she says, "Dude, man, she saw my tat. She went ballistic."

I have decided I am going to make a journal of all the words I'd like to use regularly, and "ballistic" is definitely going in there. A first-rate vocabulary makes a very good impression on people. When you have command of the English language, people admire you and sometimes they don't even know why. An excellent vocabulary has a *subliminal* effect. Gwen interrupts my thoughts with, "Dude, you got the tat! No way! Let's see!" Within seconds Justina peels down her Jordache's to reveal the image of Gumby playing a red flying-V guitar on the inside of her right thigh; her face is beaming with pride. Now *this* is good. Gwen and I both play it casual, like this is the millionth tattoo we'd seen.

"Right *on*" is Gwen's reaction. I just look at the inside of Justina's tiny thigh and try not to notice that something is off. I squint at her thigh, staring way longer than is cool or even appropriate.

"Is it blurry?" I ask finally. Gwen slaps my arm. "Shut up, you moron!"

So I do. But it is still blurry.

Justina pulls up her pants, sits on the floor, and says she needs a smoke. She pulls a pack of Marlboro Reds out of her purse and offers one to Gwen. Without skipping a beat, Gwen reaches down and takes one. I look at her like she's just licked the road to see what it would taste like, and she warns me with a pinch. I am treading on thin ice now.

Justina and Gwen each hold their cigarette in their right hand between the first two fingers, and casually flick the ashes into my mother's ashtray as if it were the most normal thing in the world to be sitting in our living room having a smoke on a school night. I watch them as they talk and use their cigarettes like little lighted pointers to enhance certain words. Gwen can blow smoke rings like a professional, and I hate to say it, but she looks so grown-up doing it. Her long, black hair is all pushed over to one side as she brings the cigarette to her mouth. She puffs—*inhales*—and then clicks her jaw in perfect rhythm to form circles of smoke in the air. That part bothers me most of all. Watching Gwen blow smoke rings is like this window onto her life I don't want to look through, but all around me I can see the changes. When Justina became her new best friend it was certainly a big change from the crowd of cheerleaders she had run with in Boonesville. But I could still pretend that Gwen was a sideliner, not really in the game. I could pretend that she was experimenting with a new crowd. Doing research, even? But somehow the smoke rings change everything. The smoke rings, in their practiced-to-perfection form, are the evidence. Gwen is a participator. And then a very scary truth comes to me. It is this: Smoke rings ain't even the half of it. Then the rest: My sister is becoming someone I don't know. Someone I may not *want* to know.

Justina looks over at me and offers the pack, but only because she knows I won't take it. Then she starts cracking up, laughing; so does Gwen. I don't feel like I should laugh too, because I think the joke is about me, so I just wait for them to stop.

Finally I say, "I used to smoke."

Gwen curls her lip and says, "You mean that time when we were little?"—like I was a complete dork.

"That *counts*," I insist.

Justina wants to hear the story, so I tell her quickly about how we'd gotten caught smoking cigarettes in Boonesville with the Kramer twins, my heart pounding the whole time because I can't believe I have the floor. Our mom had caught us in the basement trying to smoke some of the cigarette butts we'd found in the ashtray down there. She was so mad, she made us smoke a whole cigarette in front of her, and we got sick from it. The whole room was spinning, and Gwen puked, but I leave out that part because she would kill me for telling. I also leave out that we'd had to take a bath, and after our bath our mom had pulled down our pajama bottoms and spanked us harder than ever, leaving perfect pink handprints on our butts. We got sent to our rooms without dinner and waited for our dad to get home. I remember Gwen was scared, because she said our dad was gonna kill us. But when he got home and we told him, all he did was put his face in his hands and cry. Of course, I omit that part, too. I don't want Justina to think my dad is a wimp or anything.

"Dude, I gotta bail." Justina snuffs out her cigarette and stands up.

"Where to?"

"Let's go to the old mill. Tim says a bunch of them are going down there tonight."

The old mill house is an abandoned cabin on the Owens family farm. The Owens family goes back six generations in this county, and their farm is over two hundred acres. The old mill sits next to a dormant cornfield, and a tiny trickle of a stream runs past the front of it. It's only about a mile from school. I have never been there. The only kids who go there are the ones who hang out in the smoking section during Flex and Lunch, and I'm not really friends with any of them.

"Okay," Gwen says, putting out her cigarette too. "Let's go."

"Gwen! You can't go now. You'll get in trouble."

Gwen looks around the room incredulously. "With who?"

"*Mom.*"

She rolls her eyes. "Well, I don't see a mom anywhere around here, do you?"

"Well, no, but . . . what if she comes home? I'm not lying for you."

"You don't have to."

"Good."

"Because you're coming with us."

"What?"

"If you're with me, you can't tell on me. Besides, you need to live a little."

I look at Justina, ready to defend myself, but she is nodding her head. "Seriously, dude. You're getting weirder."

Gwen laughs. "Let's do it." Then she turns to me. "Do *not* act like a dork."

We exit through the window and walk around front to pile into Justina's enormous 1979 gold Cadillac. She is so small she has to sit on a phone book to see over the dash. We drive a while, then stop at a dirt road and walk the rest of the way.

There are no lights—there's no electricity—just a small bonfire burning next to the house and the glow of cigarettes floating in the dark. When we get closer I see that the house is empty, nothing but an old ratty mattress and empty beer cans everywhere. Kids are standing in small groups, just standing around in the dark corners smoking and drinking National Bohemians or Mickey's Big Mouths.

We walk through the crowd and everyone either high fives Gwen and Justina or gives them a reverent "What's up." They are famous here.

When we get inside, Justina finds Tim sitting on a mattress smoking a bowl.

"You made it!" he says, and makes room for us on the mattress. Justina fills him in on the tattoo ordeal and he takes a big hit off the bowl. "That's lame," he says, his lungs full of smoke. "Fucking lame."

He holds the bowl out to Justina and she tokes, then she holds it out to me.

"Here," she says. "This'll take the edge off."

"Are you smoking *pot*?"

A round of wheezy laughter. Justina exhales and blows all the smoke in my face. I cough and wave it away fervently while everyone laughs like I am the evening's entertainment.

A skinny guy wearing the stoner uniform—rock-concert T-shirt, jeans, and leather jacket—walks over to us. He beelines it for Gwen and greets her with a kiss. Then he whispers something in her ear and they walk off into the field.

Justina and Tim make out on the mattress and I try not to notice. I survey the room. All the guys here have the same hair, these sort of overgrown mullets, an odd kind of hair purgatory where the sides are short and the back is long. It's like they haven't really been rebelling long enough to see any real progress. Except Danesh. I recognize him from school. Danesh is Indian and has never cut his hair since birth for cultural reasons. All he had to do for acceptance was take his turban off; now he just lets it flow all wavy and black down to his waist. Oh, how the rest of the Mulletboys covet that hair! Adolescence is funny like that. One day you are a joke and the next you are something to aspire to. It's good to know, too, that a simple thing like hair can really level the playing field.

Someone has brought a boom box and is playing a tape of Judas Priest's *Defenders of the Faith*. Every time one side ends, he has to stop his conversation to cross the room and flip the tape. Before long, Gwen and Steve return and join us on the mattress. When the tape plays "Night Comes Down," Gwen asks him to go and rewind it three times in a row. And he does.

"Gwen," I say. "Mom is going to be home. We have to go."

She sighs heavily. She taps Justina, who looks at her without pulling her lips away from Tim's. "We gotta bail, dude."

They say their good-byes and we walk back down the same dirt road leading to the car. They sing Judas Priest songs and laugh all the way.

"I want Twinkies!" Justina announces. "I got the munchies."

I give Gwen the eye. We don't have time for Twinkies.

"It's a quick stop, Ellie. No big deal."

"If Mom comes home and finds us gone we are dead."

"Well, she's never home so . . . what are the odds?"

I am about to launch into my usual routine, about how I am

not a gambler and so forth, but Gwen just holds up her hand.

"You gotta chill out, dude." She puts her arm around me. "That's what's so great about having a single parent. It's very hard to keep tabs." She turns to Justina. "It's been a free-for-all since our dad split." They do a high five and walk off down the road. I linger behind while Gwen's words resonate in me. Split? He left, yes. But we saw him. At first every weekend. Then less and less, and now . . . nothing for months. My mom says he doesn't want to see us anymore. And now all I do is try to remember if maybe I did something to make that true.

After the Twinkies, when we finally get into our neighborhood, Justina idles the car around the corner so Gwen and I can climb out undetected. We head toward home in the darkness and feel around for the open window. When I am halfway over the sash, I hear our mom's car turning onto our street.

"Shit!" Gwen says, pulling me in the rest of the way.

We hear the engine shut off.

"Hurry!"

Her car door opens, closes. Then we hear her key in the door.

We don't have time to make it to our beds so we turn on the TV, dive for the couch, and pretend to be asleep. It is hard to make out her form in the dark, but I can see my mother's silhouette stagger slowly into the living room. She wobbles on her high black heels and turns off the television. She comes over to me, pulls the afghan over my legs, and puts her lips to my forehead. It is kind of like a kiss, but it is longer, and there isn't that

pucker noise to signify the end of it. But she lingers at my forehead nonetheless, and I breathe in all the smells I've come to
know as hers: Aquamarine body lotion, Winston Lights cigarettes, and, well, more than a few Bloody Marys.

four

My mother is the cleanest person you will ever meet. She is probably the cleanest person in the country, if not the world. In fact, cleanliness is her personal moral compass. She only judges a person based on whether they are clean or not. A person isn't good or bad in her book, only clean or unclean. This doesn't just pertain to personal hygiene, but, even more importantly, to the way people keep house or clean up after themselves. This is the kind of thing I'm talking about: Sometimes I can imagine a hit man in a dark suit coming into our house and killing Gwen and me, and I hate to say it, but I think that as long as he cleaned up after himself and took the trash to the curb on his way out, my mother would be forced to speak of his good points.

Every Saturday morning for as long as I can remember my mother has made Gwen and me get up at seven A.M. We spend all morning scrubbing the floors, doing laundry, and vacuuming, with bandannas tied on our heads for effect. We take turns doing the kitchen and bathrooms because we both hate those jobs equally. It's always been this way, except my mom used to clean with us. Now she sleeps until noon, just as we are finishing, and if we've done a good job and managed not to wake her up, she offers to drive us wherever we want to go. Except, "wherever we want to go" has now been augmented to include the phrase "within reason." Gwen is old enough to drive now, but she isn't allowed to get her license until she graduates because she cut school for a whole week last February.

For years Gwen and I would ask our mom to drive us to the mall. We would spend all afternoon playing Wedding. We would pretend we were getting married and go into all the dress shops and try on those beautiful white gowns. We'd take turns being the bride-to-be. When it was my turn, Gwen would wander down the rows of gowns like a frantic older sister telling the saleslady, "It has to be perfect, she must look like she stepped right off the cake! I want drama! Jewels! Sparkle!" Meanwhile, I would play along, the straight man as it were, like she was just oh-so-overbearing and I thought I was gonna explode from the stress. The saleslady and I would exchange knowing glances. I always wondered how we got away with it. I figured either we looked older than we are (and we have been told this) or the shopkeepers just thought it was too cute not to play along. After hours of searching we would decide on the perfect not-too-frilly-not-too-plain gown and place it on hold, saying we simply couldn't go forward without Mummy's approval.

After we had exhausted ourselves and every saleslady at Montgomery Park Mall, we'd go and get Cokes at the food court while we waited for our mom to pick us up. A couple months ago, while we were sipping our Cokes, I noticed Gwen surveying the food court and only half paying attention to our conversation. Her enthusiasm at Wedding was not up to par that day, either. She put up absolutely no protest when I wanted to be the bride first, and when she let me be the bride two times in a row, I knew something was amiss. At the food court, I could swear she sat farther away from me than before, but maybe I was just being sensitive. Now, instead of the mall, Gwen always wants to go to Justina's house, because Justina's mom works at a beauty parlor on Saturdays and they can lie outside by the pool without their tops on.

I don't enjoy going to the mall by myself, though sometimes I do go, and when I'm there I find myself playing what I call House, which is a bit like Wedding but different. In House, you don't have to make a big whoop-de-do and get everyone else involved like you do in Wedding. House is more personal. I started doing it one day when I knew I had an hour left before my mom would be there to get me, and I'd already been through all the clothing stores, including Contempo Casuals, *twice*.

I wandered into a furniture store called Domain that I'd never been in. The furniture in there was the most beautiful stuff you ever saw. It was all brand-new but it looked old, so at first I thought it was a used-furniture store. But then I saw the prices. The store was filled with enormous armoires and dressers with what the saleslady described as a "distressed finish." The couches were overstuffed and covered with muted linen slipcovers. The lamps all had shades of silk with beads and fringe and little personalities! I just loved it in there. It was so comfy and inviting that I found myself picturing exactly what pieces I would pick to go in my house. I was so careful in my selection, sticking to a budget and everything. Now, each time I go to the mall, I pick a different room in the house to furnish. The first room I did was the living room, which is the most practical considering it is the most used room in the house, plus the one used for company. I chose to do it in sage and cream with rose accents. I've also picked out everything I will need for the master bedroom, all in different shades of white. So many shades of white to choose from! Who knew! The bed is a large wrought-iron canopy with sheer white fabric cascading over the top and down the sides. It was hard to decide on that bed because I thought it might be too dramatic, but then I figured I'd just go for it. Next I want to decorate a sitting room, which is a small type of space where you can go to read or have tea with a friend. I'm thinking of a garden theme for that one.

Today I go into the store and spend so much time deciding on a wall quilt that I forget all about my mom picking me up until I see her charging by the store window on the hunt for me. I call for her and she comes into Domain all out of breath.

"Let's go," she says through gritted teeth. But I am so content there that I am not quite ready to compliantly follow her out.

I say, "Mommy, look at this armoire," as I point to the huge green entertainment center I've chosen for my future living room. "Isn't it breathtaking?"

My mother glances at it briefly, then turns to me, and says, "Looks like it needs a paint job. Now let's go. I'm late because of you."

I tow behind her all the way to the car. But deep down I know that the future and all the choices I've made are back there waiting for me just as I left them. And when I am ready, I can go back for them.

We get to the car and it whines a few times before turning over. The radio is already on, so when the car starts up, my mom does a little celebratory cabbage patch dance.

I pull down the visor mirror and check my face. I am rather plain looking. My eyes are green, which is more special than having blue or brown eyes. But other than that, I am not much to look at, just full cheeks and straight teeth. I have an overbite; it's not severe or anything, but one time Gwen said that when I laugh it looks like I'm going to chew off my chin. I probably should have had braces, but Gwen got them first, and I don't think there was any money left in the kitty for me.

One thing I always felt would add a little zip to my face is dimples. I once had a babysitter who promised that if I stuck my finger in my cheek and turned it every day for a year, I would get dimples. I have stuck to it and I think it is finally working. I definitely see some progress on the left. I need to share the news.

"Look!" I say. "It's been working! I'm getting a dimple!"

Mom looks while trying to keep her eyes on the road. "Where?"

"Here. On the left." I contort my face into a tight, broad smile.

"Oh, yeah. I see." But I can tell by her tone she isn't quite convinced. I check the mirror again, eye the budding dimple with suspicion.

"Are you staying home tonight?" I ask.

"No, ma'am. I have a date. Do you want Burger King?"

"Yes please and who with!"

"Ellie, honey, talk normal."

"Yes, I want Burger King, and who is your date with?" I try really hard not to, but I roll my eyes and thank God she didn't see or I would have gotten the back of her hand. She's like the Karate Kid with that thing. And she wears rings, too. When rolling one's eyes around my mother, it is always best to err on the side of caution.

Her face lights up at my interest in her date, and she says, "Reggie," as though I would automatically know exactly who she means. But I can't place the name.

"Reggie?" I say blankly. She gets annoyed briefly but doesn't want to ruin the moment since we are talking about her, so she fixes her tone and says,

"You know . . . *Reggie*."

I search in my mind for some mental snapshot I have taken. It sounds familiar but I just can't focus . . . then there it is. Back in the corner of my mind . . . a vision. A striped shirt . . . a sewed-on name tag . . . it is all becoming clear.

"The *cable guy*?" There is no hiding my horror. I brace myself for the back of her hand but she keeps both hands on the wheel. "Not everyone's a movie star, Ellie."

"I know. It's just . . . well . . . isn't he . . ."

"What? Isn't he what?"

"Isn't he . . . *black*?"

She is quiet for a moment, her eyes fixed on the road.

"He is *mixed*, actually. Miss Smart Mouth."

We drive in silence after that. As we approach the Burger King, she slows down, then she speeds back up and makes the left turn toward home. I turn to her, thinking she's forgotten to stop. But when I see the grin on her face, I know she hasn't.

"You know what your problem is?" she says. "You think your shit doesn't stink." Then she shakes her head, disgusted. "You are just like your father."

After we pull into our parking space in front of the house, my mom gives a deep sigh. Then she says, "I think I'll ask Reggie to take me to the Golden Bull tonight. Steak sounds so good, doesn't it?" She gets out of the car and hurries inside, leaving me behind. I pull down the visor mirror, force a smile. I guess it could be just a line. A dimple is definitely more of a circle than a line, if you're going to get technical about it.

I walk inside. I can hear her upstairs running a bath. Now it is just me standing alone in the kitchen. I am stuck here tonight because Gwen is with Justina, Greg has to work at the drugstore on Saturday nights, and Celia's not allowed to do *any*thing on Saturday nights because she has to get up early on Sundays for church. Sometimes her parents will let me stay over on a Saturday night, and I get up early with them and we all go to church together. But we have to plan that way in advance; it can't be a last-minute type of thing. Besides, the only time I like doing that is if it's Doughnut Sunday at the church, and that is only the first Sunday of each month. Otherwise, what's the point?

Our kitchen is sort of oldish looking, with brown and white tile and Harvest Gold appliances that were "all the go" just ten short years ago. In our kitchen, there is usually no food to be found. Ever. My mother makes two things for dinner every week: spaghetti and this other noodle dish with sausage and cabbage in it. She makes the spaghetti on Monday and we eat it until Wednesday. Then she makes the noodle thing, which we eat until Friday. On Saturdays we get Burger King or McDonald's, or even Roy Rogers if she's in a really good mood. Once, she let us get Double Roast Beefs at Roy's, then drove to McDonald's for the fries, since they have the best ones. She even let us get apple pies that time.

I probably shouldn't have said Reggie was black. That was rude. Or maybe she was already mad because I was in Domain so long. No, because she still asked me if I wanted to go to Burger King *after* we got in the car, so she still intended to take me at that point. At least I think that's how it went. I'll have to try to remember it better later on.

My thoughts are interrupted by my growling stomach. I look in the refrigerator and find the following items: one large tub of Country Crock butter, mayonnaise, Wonder Bread, a tomato. And a pitcher of instant iced tea.

The doorbell rings and I open the door to find a tall, slender man with creamy coffee-colored skin and a bald head. His nose is mushy-looking and flat. He reminds me of a younger, lighter Bill Cosby, minus the hair. When he sees me standing there he says, "You must be Ellie." The first thing I notice is that he is holding a Dunkin' Donuts bag in his hand. It is crumpled and stained, a bit worse for wear. He sees me looking at it and asks where the trash is.

He follows me into the kitchen and I show him the trash can. He steps on the little lever that makes the lid go up. "Been in my truck for days," he says, and drops the bag into the can.

I tell him he should sit because my mom's not ready yet.

"Oh. That's fine. Just fine." I feel bad for him suddenly because he seems nervous and I'm not saying much. I keep expecting him to start talking about Jell-O pudding and I'm hurting for small talk, so I ask him if anyone's ever told him he looks like Bill Cosby, and before he can answer me I hear my mother's heels clicking in the hall.

My mother is wearing a white wrap dress with shoulder pads and brown high-heeled sandals, her beaded clutch in one hand. She has pink blush right on the apples of her cheeks. Usually I am taller than she is; right now we are the same height. Her hair is very short and colored a nearly platinum blond. She went gray at twenty-eight, she says, because of us kids. Reggie sees her come around the corner and smiles like he can't believe his luck. She smiles back, the kind of smile I haven't seen in months. They hug with a familiarity that makes me look away.

"So. You met?" Reggie and I nod in agreement. "We should go, then."

They are going about the business of leaving and I realize, *Wait, what about dinner?* I give her the look without saying the words. She checks her manicure and says quickly, with a lot of breath, "Is there something you wanted to say?"

"Yes. I'm hungry. What am I supposed to do about food?"

"Well," she says, "you should have thought of that earlier, before you got so smart."

"So I'm not eating tonight?"

She walks back into the kitchen and says in a voice just low enough so that Reggie won't hear, "You know, Ellie, I love you because you are my daughter. But sometimes I really don't like you very much." She turns to Reggie. "Shall we?" And they are gone.

When I was younger I used to help my mother with dinner. My favorite thing to make was lasagna. There was an exactly right way of doing it, the layering, so that each new layer fit perfectly on the one beneath it. Sauce first, then noodles, then cheese filling; repeat. If you weren't careful, you could use up all the filling or the sauce before you were done, then the whole thing would be off. You had to watch that.

Maybe it's selective memory, but I know it wasn't always this hard with us. And it wasn't just lasagna. It was lots of things. Gwen has always had more friends than me, so when she was away for a sleepover, my mom and I would have our own slumber party. She would make popcorn on the stove and we'd watch *Dallas*. During commercial breaks she'd turn the radio on and we would dance in our pajamas. I could even jump on the bed if the music moved me to it. She always laughed. Always. Every time.

Then she was just sad all the time, and now if she's still sad, she hides it behind something else. My dad wasn't home when we had slumber parties, and before he left he hardly talked at all. We could hear them arguing—first the yelling, then the muffled conversations behind their bedroom door. Gwen would listen on the stairs, but I never wanted to. I would go get her, beg her to finish playing Barbies. We spent hours setting up the houses, picking out the clothes, and choosing jobs for Barbie and Ken, then she wouldn't want to play. She'd just sit on the stairs and listen to them fight. One time I asked her how she could sit there and listen to that, and she said, "How can you *not*?"

I watch TV for two hours, but all that is on is food commercials and people eating. They are eating pizza, mostly, and cookies, and they are laughing while they do it. Then I remember: the Dunkin' Donuts bag. Once the thought is in my head I cannot make it leave. It teases me. It calls me. It becomes an act I must complete. I go to the trash and retrieve the bag. Inside, four slightly melted and very smooshed chocolate-covered dough-nuts. Wait. Is that cream filling?

I sit down at the table and breathe them in. Deeply. I reach into the bag and eat—no, inhale—the first one. It is so good, but it is gone too quickly. I stand up, take out the next one. Now I am leaning against the counter. I eat the doughnut so fast I hardly get to taste it. I retrieve the next one, play a game as to how many bites it takes to finish. Five. I eat the last one, slowing down a bit now, stopping to smell it between bites. I reach into the bag; it is empty, but I am not ready to stop. I open the refrigerator and pull out the bread and margarine. I butter a slice of bread like I am in a hurry. I mush it in my fist until it makes a little ball, then I pop it into my mouth. Then another. And then another. Then the rest of the bread. The room is spinning; I am dizzy. And I am sick, I am so sick. But it is better. That feeling, the one that wouldn't go away, is gone now. I am pleasantly numb. I have a feeling of completion. I unbutton my pants and lie down on the couch, digest it all.

five

sunday morning around ten, I'm still in bed, hanging upside down over the side letting all the blood rush to my head. My whole head feels like one, big, tight throbbing. This feeling draws me and repels me at the same time. I wonder if my eyes will pop out if I never sit back up. Luckily, the phone rings. I sit up.

"Hello?" I say, half conscious, as the blood starts returning to all the right places.

"Hey, it's me." *Celia.*

"How was church?" Though I don't really care.

"Uh . . . *snore.* We're going to the mall. Wanna come? I have to buy a purse."

I was just at the mall yesterday, but the alternative is to continue my eye-popping experiment, so I say, "I gotta ask. Hang on."

I put the phone to my chest and call downstairs. I can hear her in the kitchen but she won't answer me because she hates when I yell down to her, which I always forget. I walk down the stairs to the first landing and say as loudly as I can without yelling, "Mom? Can I go to the . . ."

"I'm not driving you!" *That* was a yes. I run back to the phone.

"You can come get me, right?"

"Yep."

"See ya in twenty?"

Well, how about that. Suddenly, I have plans. It was going to be another boring Sunday stretched out in front of me, and now I am going to the mall with my best friend to help her pick out a purse. She really values my opinions on things like that. For homecoming she was going to buy a black off-the-shoulder dress, but I was able to steer her toward the red. She was the hit of the dance. Celia tends to go the safer route with her accessories as well, buying classics, whereas I believe accessories should showcase your personality. Today, I will do my part to help.

I decide to wear my jeans with the zippers at the ankles and a pink-and-white-striped tank top. I have shoes that look like MIAs: flat and pointed with tiny silver studs on them. Except they're not MIAs at all. We got them at a discount mall up near the Pennsylvania border, and I gotta say, they look like the real thing. The only problem is, they're not real leather, so it was hard to break them in at the beginning of the school year. By seventh period on the first day I had an unfortunate limp,

because my right heel had a blister so bad I just started dragging my foot to protect it from the friction of all that heel-toe-
heel-toe motion.

I can hear my mother in her bedroom now. She is not alone;
their whispers and occasional laughter carry softly down the
hall. I go out the front door and sit on the stoop to wait for
Celia.

Celia does not come over to my house anymore except when
her parents pick me up and drop me off. At the beginning of
the school year, when our friendship was new, I invited her to
spend the night. My mother was driving to Virginia to see my
grandmother and would be away until Sunday. Gwen had
invited Justina, and I wanted to show off my new friend too.

Unbeknownst to me, Gwen had decided that we couldn't let
an unsupervised weekend go to waste, so she invited most of
the junior class over for a party. Two hours after my mother
left, Celia and I were helping to party-proof the house, putting
all of Mom's Hummels out of reach while Gwen and Justina
pumped the keg. I was laughing about something, Hummel in
hand, when my mother just walked in the front door. She had
forgotten her checkbook.

I heard Justina say, *Oh, shit* . . . and that was it. Without a
word, my mother charged. She grabbed both Gwen and Justina
by the hair. "What do you think you're doing?" Justina managed to wrestle herself away. Gwen stayed put; her head jerked
back, exposing her throat. My mother let her go and began
breaking all of Gwen's record albums, one by one. She broke
them over the bookcase and over the banister, leaving little

black shards all over the room. "Now clean this up!" she yelled, and ran up to her room. We could hear her crying on the phone, telling our grandma why she couldn't come visit. I remember her shouting, "I hate them!" as loud as I've ever heard her, and thinking, *My God, she means it.*

When Celia and Mrs. Meyers pull up, I am ready to go. I get in the backseat and Celia gets out of the front passenger seat and comes to sit in back with me. I always feel bad for Mrs. Meyers, sitting up there all alone like she's our chauffeur or something. But she plays along and even speaks in a phony British accent sometimes.

Celia is all wound up about church and how she had to sit next to Monica Pinsky, who smells like B vitamins. She says she's sick of church and she's not going anymore. When she says, "Do you hear that Mom? I'm not going!" Mrs. Meyers says, in her British accent, "Sorry, m' lady, I am just the driver. I know nothing of it," and winks at me in the rearview mirror. Celia just rolls her eyes.

"I'm in love," I announce out of nowhere. Celia is boy-crazy, so this gets her attention.

"Oh?" Then she says louder, for her mother to hear, "*See.* Look at all I am missing!" As though my love life ebbs and flows during the exact hours she is at church.

Mrs. Meyers ignores her. "Who's the lucky boy, Ellie?"

Celia says, "I thought you were just the driver!" Instinctively, I brace for something. Some kind of impact. Some kind of consequence. But it never comes. I just see Mrs. Meyers shake her head. Celia turns to me and sighs heavily. *"Anyway.* You were *saying?"*

"Oh. Yes . . . I love Elvis Presley!" And my smile is so big that I have to stretch my bottom lip off my teeth, making my neck look strained, just to convey it all.

Celia looks utterly defeated and throws herself against the back of the car seat. "I thought you meant for real this time."

Celia is referring to my habit of loving the unattainable. Celia and I have both had a string of crushes, which is perfectly normal for our age. However, her crushes have been Mike Cady, who sits next to her in Lab Science; Ronald Shuman, who rides the bus to school with her; Todd Stevens, who works in the attendance office third period and also lives next door to her; and a mild obsession with Andrew, the guy from another high school who sells mulch to her mother. For Celia, that is about as exotic as it gets. For my part, my crushes have been Mr. Strauss, my history teacher last semester; John Keats, the poet; Abraham Lincoln, president extraordinaire; and now Mr. Elvis Aaron Presley, the king of rock 'n' roll himself.

Last night, after I was drunk with food, I watched a TV movie called *Elvis and Me.* It was all about the love affair of Elvis Presley and Priscilla Beaulieu. It was, hands down, the most amazing story I have ever encountered. Priscilla was just a girl, fourteen like me, when they met. They connected instantly, and she would go to school and fall asleep in class because she had been up all night with him, just talking. And when her parents wanted her to stop seeing him, Elvis himself came over to their house, in his uniform and everything, hat in hand. He asked for permission to keep seeing her, and of course they couldn't say no. He is Elvis Presley.

Elvis wanted to fly Priscilla to Graceland for a visit, and her parents said no, flat out. But she said, "You can't *stop* me." Just like that. She didn't even have to raise her voice; that is how much she meant it. And you know what? They didn't stop her. When they wouldn't let her go to Los Angeles to see him, she locked herself in her room for days and wouldn't come out. That part really shocked me. One time, my mother was chasing me up the stairs and I ran into my room and locked the door behind me. She was banging so hard it scared me more, so I figured I may as well open the door and get it over with. She came at me with her arms flailing wildly, open hands, fists, all of her, just striking me wherever she could get. I remember I curled myself into a little ball and just waited for it to stop. Priscilla, on the other hand, never opened her door. She turned it around on them. Her parents were begging and pleading *her* before it was all over. You see, Elvis's love made her strong. It filled her up completely, then protected her like armor. And then it picked her up and carried her away.

Celia jumps into her crushes full on, getting into relationships and everything. She even scribbles her signature with the guy's last name. Celia *Cady*. I had to agree, it sounded pretty good, although Celia *Stevens* sounded best. I envy that part of her. The part that can be so easily satisfied with what is in front of her. When she was in her third relationship of the school year (and it is annoying when she is in a relationship because every Flex and Lunch period is spoken for by New Guy), I said she was becoming a serialist. But she just sighed impatiently and said, "Can I help it if I keep finding love?" That is what I am talking about. Love, right next to you, a couple of times a year. It is something.

Uninterested in hearing about my love for Elvis, Celia asks—no, *tells*—her mother to turn on the radio. Wham is on, "Careless Whisper." Celia and Todd's song.

"Can you push the first button?" she calls to the front. Mrs. Meyer does. Tears for Fears. "Shout." I kind of like that song, but Celia curls her lip.

"Can you push two?" It goes to talk radio. "I said *two*! Jesus!" She looks at me like, *Can you believe this?* Her nostrils flare at the injustice.

Her mom pushes the second preset button and says in her normal voice, "Please watch your tone, Celia. Okay?" Celia looks at me and cocks her head to the side. She says, *"Fine,"* and rolls her eyes.

I can't help thinking what a funny age this is and how Celia and I are always trying to save face with one another. The way Celia is speaking to her mother is her way of showing off to me. Celia is so aware of the lines drawn around her; it is her duty to test them, and to be embarrassed when she is corrected for them. She has turned to me for support in the unfairness of her correction, so I give her a knowing smile and roll my eyes like she wants me to. But, what I am thinking is how much easier that would be . . . a line so clearly drawn, you knew when you were overstepping, and when you got in trouble, well, you'd know exactly what you had done wrong.

"Turn it up! Wooohoooo!" Celia has recovered and we are in bliss as Simon Le Bon belts out, *"The reflex is a lonely child, who's waiting by the paaaark!"* Mrs. Meyers giggles as Celia and I bob our heads in perfect rhythm, turning to each other at the exact right moment for when he says, "Fle-flex," like we are in the video. We are laughing hysterically; my sides start to hurt from it and Celia puts her hand up to me like, *Stop,* which, of course, makes us laugh even harder. Celia's good like that, even if she doesn't realize she has the best mother in the whole world.

Mrs. Meyers drops us off outside of Hecht's and gives Celia money for her purse. Celia is all business today. She wants a Le Sport Sac purse but she can't decide on size or color. She is mainly concerned with it matching her backpack, which is red. I tell her she doesn't always have her backpack with her so we don't have to limit ourselves. She just sighs and says, "I have it all day, five days a week, don't I?" And I don't get mad because she is right.

It takes all of five minutes for Celia to find the purse she wants. Despite my argument for the cute deep pink bag, she buys the khaki one. She pays the saleslady and says, "Let's get fries." But when we get to the food court, I tell her I don't have any money. "That's okay. I'll pay." It's quick the way she says it. I don't know if it means anything, but I hear myself say I've been thinking about getting a job.

"You're too young to work."

"I am?"

"You have to be fifteen. But you could babysit. Do you want a drink, too?" I say no, but I do.

We sit in the food court and eat our fries. We each open one of those little salts and sprinkle it over the pile. Across the court we see Kevin Lasky from school. He's a very big deal, basketball team and all that, and Celia has homeroom with him. The gift of the alphabet, she says. I personally don't see what the big deal is. I mean, okay, sure: blond hair, blue eyes, tall, muscle-y body. He glances over and finds us gawking, then gives Celia a nod of acknowledgment. She does a quick, flapping wave with her fingertips and turns to me for approval. I smile with just the side part of my mouth.

"What?" she asks me. But I don't have an answer. I'm thinking, *He's probably next.* And there you are. Flex and Lunch alone for the rest of the year.

"My mom won't be here for another hour," Celia says. "Let's look around."

I tell her there is nothing new at Contempo, and I should know since I was just there yesterday. Instead we go into Woodies Department Store. A girl who is spraying perfume on little cards stops us. She asks us if we'd like to try Eternity, the new Calvin Klein fragrance, and when she waves the card around to dry it, I notice there are wet stains under both her armpits. Spraying perfume must be harder than it looks.

Celia and I head to the makeup counter and try on all the new stuff. Lancôme has a spring color collection that has pastel yellow, green, and pink eye shadows in it. They also have a mauve lipstick that is perfect and smells like roses. I am the first one to reach the counter and I get to work. The saleslady comes over and asks if she can help me, but I'm doing just fine, so I say no.

"I mean, do you want to *buy* anything?"

"I'm just sampling for now, thanks."

She considers this a moment, then walks away to help another customer. I continue trying out the makeup, doing different variations on each eyelid with my fingers, designating one color per finger so the colors stay true. I survey my artistry in the mirror. Lipstick will complete the look. I pick up a tube of Mauvelous lipstick and swipe the bluish pink shade across my lips.

In the mirror, I see Celia trying on a chalky pink lipstick like all the girls at school wear. Our eyes meet. "It's great, right?" And it is. "Especially with lots of electric blue eyeliner." She has a trick where she sticks her eyeliner on her hot curling iron to get more color out of it. I agree, and watch her as she calls the saleslady over, points to her lips, and gets her wallet out. Simple. Here. I want this. Done.

Before I know what I am doing, I am sticking lipsticks into my pockets. I make sure to grab the Mauvelous. I put a bottle of Paris perfume in my purse and pull the Spring Collection eye shadows from the Velcro holder on the display, finding room in my pocket for them, too. My heart is in my throat. I stop to look around and see the saleslady handing Celia her change and a little foil bag.

Celia comes over to me. "Ready?" She pauses a minute, takes me in. "Wow. Those eye shadows look great on you." But my heart is beating so loud I hardly hear her. Suddenly, the shadows are burning a hole in my pocket. I want to say, *Celia, help me,* but I just walk faster. Celia wants to know what the hurry is, and again I have no answer. Just put one foot in front of the other. The door is just over there. But I get to walking so fast that I don't notice the trail of lipsticks I am leaving behind.

Then I hear the heels clicking on the glassy floor, the *swish-swish* of panty hose.

"Excuse me!" Faster and faster, coming up behind us. Celia slows to turn, and I grab her arm.

"Do not turn around." I am grinding my teeth hard. I hear the footsteps quickening. The saleslady yells, "Girls! Stop!" Celia searches my face for some kind of explanation, but there is no time.

"Run!" I yell at her, but it stuns her and she stops. "Run now! Celia! Run!"

And we are off. We are running at full throttle, my pockets clamoring. We run out the front entrance of the department store and out to the parking lot. We do not stop running until we get to the bushes on the other side of the street. The saleslady is gone. I collapse onto the grass behind the bushes. Celia does too. She is completely out of breath like me.

"Ellie? What. The. Hell?" She puts her head between her knees to compose herself, and I see a security car cruising around the parking lot.

"Get down!"

"Goddamn it! *What?*"

I am thinking that for once she should just shut up, because we are in very big trouble.

"I stole stuff. I stole makeup. The lady saw me. Get down!"

"Oh, for Christ's sake, *Ellie.*" She says my name like it tastes bad or something. "This is just *great.*" And I see it on her face:

something resembling regret. Like maybe when she became friends with me she hadn't known what she was getting herself into.

I stick my head back up to check for the security car and see Mrs. Meyers's car pulling into the lot.

"Your mom's here!"

"Thank *God*."

I see the security car disappear around the far corner of the building, away from us. On three, we run as fast as we can to the car. Mrs. Meyers is putting on lipstick in the mirror and doesn't see from which direction we came.

Celia rides up front this time. Mrs. Meyers wants to have a look at the purse.

"Couldn't talk her into the colored one, huh, Ellie?"

"No, ma'am. I couldn't." Then I realize that I am like that Eddie Haskell guy. No, *worse*.

It's silent for a moment, and Mrs. Meyers senses the tension.

"Is everything all right?"

Neither of us say anything. I can hear my heart thumping between my ears.

"Celia? I'm talking to you."

Celia keeps her eyes fixed ahead. "Everything's fine."

Mrs. Meyers decides to leave it alone. "All right, then," she says, and drives out of the lot.

I stay quiet, not sure which is more real: my nausea or my relief. I feel around in my bulging pockets; I want to look at what's in there, see what I can do now. My hands are still shaking, so I look down at them, then at the traffic. The cars are going by, people are just driving along like everything is the same. But, oh, are they wrong.

We pull up to my townhouse; ours is the last in the row. A coveted end unit. There is a white van parked in one of the spaces out front. Some guy I have never seen is carrying a hose over to it.

Celia, her mom, and I say our silent good-byes, then I grab my lumpy purse and climb out of the car.

As I get out, I hear music pumping from the van. Aerosmith. From where I am, the van guy is kind of scruffy looking: Tall and muscle-thin, faded jeans, a black T-shirt with the sleeves cut off, a tattoo of an eagle or something on his shoulder, no shoes. His hair is dark brown, but the ends are faded like he's been in the sun. It's wavy and long, to the top of his shoulders all the way around. He does not have an overgrown mullet. His hair is the kind that shows a real long-term commitment to being on the fringe.

I try to scoot past him and onto the sidewalk. Just as I'm about to pass, the hose starts shooting out water. I get that same uh-oh feeling I get when I pass a group of boys in a snowball fight, so I turn to him and put my hand on my hip so he knows I mean business. My stare says, *No funny stuff.*

"How ya doing?" he says, and nods up at me in acknowledgment.

How am I doing? Well. Let's see. I'm a criminal, my best friend hates me, and my mother's got jungle fever. You?

"I'm fine."

He just stands there, hose in hand, water flailing everywhere. I look down at my faux MIAs, which are getting splattered. I take my right hand, which is the one that is not on my hip, and point to my feet.

"Do you mind?" I mean, *really.*

He releases the nozzle lever and drops the hose on the sidewalk. He takes two steps toward me, stops, and just stares.

Now that he's closer, I can see his face better. He's that combination of pretty and handsome, with deep brown eyes and a tiny fleck of a mole under the right one. His eyebrows are thick and his lips are full, the bottom one slightly fuller than the top. His cheekbones are noticeably high, which is the kind of thing you only see in movie stars. He has a small silver hoop earring in his left ear. He raises his left eyebrow perfectly, like I've got a secret he wants to know.

"What's your name?" he says.

I hesitate and I'm not sure why. I suddenly need my name to sound better than it does.

"I'm Ellie." I extend my hand and he shakes it in that way that tells me he's been to lots of different places: firm, with eye contact and just a tiny squeeze.

"Hello, Ellie. I'm Leo." Without letting my hand go, he says, "Did I get your shoes wet?"

"Um. Yes. Yes, you did."

"Right. Well, sorry about that."

"Oh. Well. That's okay."

He winks at me. "You'll live, right?"

"Sure."

He lets go of my hand and I'm suddenly aware of how empty it is. All that air passing through my fingers. He just keeps staring at me, and all I can think is, *Dear God, do I have a booger hanging?* I feel like I have to say more, but I can't think of anything.

Finally I say, "Where did you come from?" and immediately wish the sidewalk would open up and swallow me. Or perhaps a UFO could be so kind as to interrupt by flying over. An alien with big black eyes could come out and say, *Ellie, you really should see this,* and I'd say, *Well, I better go—I mean how often do you get this kind of opportunity?* I'm sure this Leo guy would understand.

"Well," he says, "my parents live across the street." He points to the blue townhouse directly across from mine.

"Oh. Are you visiting?"

"You could say that."

"How long will you be here?"

"I don't know. As long as it takes, I guess."

Of course I want to ask him more. Like, what does *as long as it takes* mean, for one. As long as what takes? But already I am aware of that space in him that he is protecting. I have that space too. The one that is difficult and remote, accessible only by a very long and winding road whose shoulders are peppered with brightly colored signs that warn those attempting this road to just take it easy, slow down, and proceed with caution. It isn't that the space is totally inaccessible. It's just that, if you want to get there, you need patience, determination, and a lot of snack foods, because it is going to take a long, long time. And there's nothing worse than some jerk flying over the speed limit and disobeying all the traffic signs.

"Well, I guess I should go inside now, let you get back to washing your tan. I mean your *van*."

"Yeah, okay."

He picks up the hose and goes back to work. I force my legs to turn and walk toward my house.

With the door closed safely behind me, I am suddenly in a very good mood. I feel lighter, like if I were someone else I would hum a show tune or something. I absentmindedly check the fridge, contents undesirable as usual, so I head up to my room. Celia should be home now, so I pick up the phone to tell her about Leo. But then I remember earlier and all that happened.

I put the phone back down and spread out on my bed. There is a warmth rising up in me. Some feeling I don't recognize. I hear the hose splashing outside my window, the music cranking. I'm thinking I'd like to go back outside with some of my cassettes. Maybe he could play those, too, and after he was done washing the van we could sit on the hood and listen to them together. Maybe we'd just listen while the sun went down and talk some too. But mostly our voices would be soft. And there would be some laughter now and then.

S I X

It is monday morning and we are in the car on the way to school. I am in the backseat as usual. Gwen is in front because she calls it first every time. She's sneaky about it, too. I'll be leaning over the sink, spitting out the toothpaste, and she'll say, "I get the front seat," just like that, out of nowhere.

They are arguing, she and my mother. Gwen wants to go to Justina's house after school, but her room isn't clean.

"And? What's your point?"

"Watch your *mouth*." My mother grinds her teeth hard.

In general, Gwen does not treat authority figures with what I would call respect. Especially our mother. For our mother, her contempt is tangible, like this thing she is waving brazenly, saying, *Look at this!* She is always being sent to the principal's office for dress-code violations. Today she is wearing skintight black stretch pants and a lime green tank top, her lacey black bra clearly visible. They told her at school she had to start wearing one, so this is her way. This is how she does it. Her whole way of being is a big middle finger to the other guy.

"Just tell me why I can't go. Give me a *reason*."

"Because I'm your mother. That's why."

A pause. Then a kind of snort-laugh thing. Careful, Gwen. "Yeah," she says, "some mother." Well, that did it. My mother's hand goes flying off the steering wheel and the back of it smashes into Gwen's face. She continues to hold it up as a warning of more to come. Gwen is stone-faced. She won't even flinch. My mother returns her hand to the wheel, oblivious to the slowing cars around us. Gwen whips her head around to me. Her top lip is swollen and bleeding just a little. It's that ring with the mound of sapphires—it really does a job.

"Isn't she *great*? Dontcha *love* her?" I see her chin wiggle a little. There is more than sarcasm there, but she hides it.

My mother is steel. "Fix your face, smartass. We're almost there."

And because we are almost there, Gwen is especially brave.

"Oh, no. I want everyone to see what a wonderful mother you are."

I am so compelled to touch her, or to cry for her, *something*. But there is this other place she goes when this happens. She does not want comfort. She wants to hold it in and nurse it until the pain becomes a rage so big and full it can survive out here on its own, without me. Without anyone.

We pull to the drop-off lot at school and get out of the car. She does not care if she has to walk around like that; she will hold her head high and wear it like a red badge of courage.

She rushes into school, leaving me behind.

I am nervous all day about history class, when I will see Celia. I imagine she has told her mother all about me, about what I really am underneath. By the time sixth period comes, I have a stomachache. Celia walks in and avoids my eyes; she takes her seat, which is right next to mine. She is wearing the chalky pink lipstick. I am wearing the Mauvelous, and the shame shivers up around me like a sudden, unexpected chill. *Celia,* I want to say. *I am sorry for all I am. All that I've become. Please understand. I just want so much. I just* want *so much.*

Mr. Finkle is talking about the Civil War, and since I am over my crush on Honest Abe, it is hard to concentrate, especially with all that is going on. With my peripheral vision I see Celia taking notes, but then she taps my arm and turns her notebook toward me. In the margin she has scribbled a picture of Abe Lincoln, hat, beard, and everything, but with an exaggerated muscle-man body. I cover my mouth so as not to laugh out loud, then write quickly in my notebook, "Soooo hot!" and turn it toward her. She reads it with her hand over her mouth just in case. She doesn't make it hard for me, and for that I am grateful.

We walk down the same hall for seventh period, and I am careful not to say too much. The ice is not necessarily thick enough for skating. I do say I'm sorry, and she just nods like she knows. We are quiet again, then she says, "Ellie. Elvis Presley is dead. You have to stop liking dead people."

"Mr. Straus wasn't dead."

"He's a forty-year-old history teacher. He may as well be. "

We smile, but then her face changes.

"Ellie," she says, and her voice is so soft I want to cry, but I never would. Not in front of her. Then she says carefully, "Kevin Lasky asked me out. And his friend likes you. He saw us at the mall yesterday. We could all . . . ya know . . . go on a date?"

For a moment I can almost picture it, the four of us together, me and Celia winking at each other, knowingly, when one of the guys does something that we can discuss between us when they are not around. We are comfortable with each other that way.

"Who's the guy?"

She is relieved by my interest. "Arnie Swallows." She says it with a straight face, too, like it isn't even funny. I have to call her on it.

"Celia!"

"What?"

I search her face. I actually don't think it had registered.

"Arnie *Swallows?*"

"Oh!" She gets it suddenly and laughs so hard she has to brace herself against me.

"What are ya trying to do to me here?" I say it with an affected New York accent so she'll keep laughing. I just love it when she loses it.

The warning bell rings, so she gathers herself. Smoothing out her skirt, she asks me if I'll at least think about it. Conceding a bit, I ask how old he is.

"He's fifteen."

She is already on her way down the math hall so I have to shout now.

"He doesn't even *drive*?"

"*So?*" I see her shaking her head, just like her mother does, all the way down the hall.

It is eleven o'clock and I am in my room doing homework when I hear the front door open. Gwen is home finally. My mother emerges from her bedroom and I hear her footsteps fade down the stairs. Some part of me shrinks into a little ball and looks for a place to hide, but there is no place small enough. No place safe.

In no time, there is shouting and I hear the familiar sentences, the words meant to hurt in a way hands cannot.

"You look like a whore! Look at you!" My mother's voice carries out of the living room, into my room, out the window, and into the world.

"Well, I learned from the best, didn't I?" Then the slap, loud and hard. The way Gwen is, it is too much sometimes. It is too bold. I need to run from it, but at the same time I need to keep an eye peeled to make sure I don't miss anything.

"I am leaving here! For good!" She is crying now.

"Hallelujah!"

"I am going to live with Dad!"

"He doesn't *want* you!"

The last time we saw our dad, we spent the weekend at his new house in Aberdeen, which is about two hours away. At first he had an apartment close by in Silver Spring, but then he moved. He was all excited for us to see his new place. I was excited too, although I couldn't help but notice its proximity. Or lack of.

He had picked us up in his new car, a silver two-seater with a T-top; Gwen and I both got the front seat that time. By the end of the weekend, Gwen would call dibs on getting the window seat and I would sit painfully sandwiched in the middle. Our mother called us every hour we were there, asking what we were doing and what his apartment looked like. She told us to look for evidence of another woman.

Our dad was pretty much the same as always, though quieter than I remembered and less strict. We cooked frozen pizzas for lunch and dinner, and when we went to Erol's Video he let us rent *Rock 'n' Roll High School*, which has an R rating. He'd gotten one of those big rear-projection TVs, and we watched it two times in a row.

While Gwen snooped around for evidence of a girlfriend, I looked for evidence of another kind. I needed some kind of hard proof that he didn't, in fact, *want* us. The house was small, a one-bedroom. His car, merely a two-seater. Whether he wanted us or not was unclear, but what I did know for sure is that there simply wasn't room. And if by chance even that weren't true, I was too afraid to ask.

Gwen, on the other hand, found a peach-colored silk blouse hanging in the closet. After everyone was asleep, she opened the closet door and with scissors cut the blouse into a hundred little pieces. We left the next day, all three of us crammed in the car in awkward silence.

My mother demanded to know why we were home early, and when Gwen told her what she'd done I swear I saw the corners of her mouth turn upward in satisfaction. There was no punishment for this particular offense, no consequences . . . at least not the kind you can see right away. But for Gwen, a corner had been turned, and we all knew it.

Downstairs, the argument continues. No words now, just Gwen's choking sobs and the silence when she absorbs a blow. I can hear them, my mother's arms whipping around, the punch, smack, and pull of it all, so violent and unspecific.

I lie in my bed, frozen, humming softly to myself. From earlier today, I play it over in my head: Celia walking down the hall, me watching her go.

"How old is he?"

"He's fifteen."

"He doesn't even *drive*?" I say again.

"*So?*" She says.

Only now I think: *So . . . if he doesn't drive, how can he take me from here?*

I hear Gwen's bedroom door slam shut, wait for the footsteps that will follow her. But there are none. I exhale, breathe in the quiet. I go to her door, knock softly, then open it. It is futile to wait for an invitation. She is lying facedown in the bed. The light is on; it stuns my eyes a little, so I wait for them to adjust.

Gwen rolls over, looks at me. Her eyes are swollen from crying, and from the rest of it. Her lip is bruised now from this morning.

"I hate her." I want to say I hate her too, but I can't; though sometimes that is what it feels like. I don't get in there like Gwen does. I just circle around the outside, looking for a soft spot. I think you have to stand toe-to-toe with someone to know if you hate them. I have not done that, so I can't say. Gwen has earned her hatred, pure and true.

She sits up and pats the bed for me to sit next to her. Before I get there, the front door slams shut. We hear her get in the car, drive away.

"Gee," Gwen says with sarcastic perfection, "wonder where *she's* going." Her face is so swollen, the beauty is all squished up and hiding.

"Off to see Mr. Café Au Lait, I'm sure."

Gwen cocks her head to the side a little, not sure she heard me right. "Did you say . . . Oh, Ellie! Ha!" It worked. She is laughing, just like that. "Café Au Lait! Ah ha ha. . . ."

"Well. He *is*." Now I am laughing too. Gwen wipes tears from her eyes, ones from before, and new ones from laughing.

"Did you see his underwear?" she asks. And I did. Yesterday, before I left for the mall with Celia, my mother's bedroom door was open a bit. They were bikinis. Purple.

"You mean the grape smugglers?"

Gwen is howling now. She lays her hand on my arm, gives it a gentle push.

"The banana hammock!"

And that is it. We are writhing on the bed. Loud, achy laughter. Every time we try to gather ourselves, we give a big sigh at the exact same moment and it makes us start all over again. Gwen's head is thrown back, her mouth gaping open, her green eyes shining. She is prettier than me. I hope she knows it. She holds her stomach, and I can tell it hurts, how hard she's laughing. I put the cordless phone in my underwear and pretend I'm Reggie so she won't stop. She roars again, claps her hands in delight. "You're killing me!" she says.

There she is, I think to myself. My *sister.* A brief resuscitation.

Later, in bed, I am thinking about Elvis. He sent Priscilla to an all-girls Catholic high school in Memphis when she finally came to live with him. If that were me, I'd ask Elvis if Gwen could come too. She'd hate it, of course, especially the uniforms, and I don't know if Elvis would do it. He may want me all to himself. But I would definitely ask.

seven

I am on my front stoop again. This time I am waiting for Mrs. Davis. She wants me to call her Shelley, but I am not ready. This week I decided to join the employed. I answered an ad in the Rockshire *Gazette*: *Babysitter wanted. Weekends only. 14 & up. Will provide transportation.* That was the big seller. When I called Mrs. Davis, we hit it off right away. She said how about Friday and I said yes, not even knowing if I had plans. But you have to do it like that when you have a job. Make it your priority.

She picks me up in a big silver car. The seats are black leather and everything smells new. She is younger than I'd thought, maybe in her early twenties, which is young to have a child, but you never know how these things go. She is dressed in a light pink short-sleeved sweater, long, frothy skirt with some sort of paisley print, and flat shoes. She has dark brown bobbed hair and thin lips. She uses her hands a lot when she talks, even though she is driving, and she has a young person's voice. Her inflection rises at the end of each sentence, so every-thing she says kind of sounds like a question. "Okay. So. Taylor has to be in bed by seven?" She is very nice. I can definitely call her Shelley.

When we get there, I meet her husband, Rob. He shows me around their house, which is huge. They have wood on their floors and lights that are built into the ceiling like little glowing cans. The kitchen is so shiny it's like a commercial, and it has a pantry you can walk into. Rob says I can help myself to what-ever I want.

Shelley comes downstairs with Taylor in her arms. He is only fifteen months old. He is wearing yellow terry-cloth pajamas and just a few feathery blond hairs on his little head.

"Taylor?" Shelley says in that high baby-talk voice. "This is Ellie. Say hi, say hi, say *hello*." She bounces him a little.

I say hi and wave, though I am less than two feet away. He just stares ahead. But it's not personal; that's just the way babies are.

After they leave I am alone with Taylor. It is a weird thing; I am responsible for this . . . child. And he doesn't really do much. I set him in his playpen and turn on the TV. Then, remembering the pantry, I help myself to a few Oreos. Taylor sees me at the pantry and holds up his little hand, makes a grunting noise. I put an Oreo into my mouth. He stands him-self up in his playpen, holds on to the side, and makes his grunting more urgent.

"You want a cookie? Hmm? Is that what you want?" I am doing the baby voice too now.

"But not an Oreo." I make a funny face. "Yucky!" He laughs.

I go to the pantry and find a box of animal crackers, pull out an elephant, and hand it to him. He is happy. And I am good at this.

When it is almost seven o'clock, I boil the bottle like Shelley showed me and take Taylor upstairs. I am supposed to rock him while he has his bottle, so I sit in the rocking chair and hold him in my arms like I have seen it done. It seems like a very natural thing, being a mother. The baby comes out and they hand it to you all red and screaming, and suddenly it is all you have ever known.

Taylor helps me hold the bottle and stares at me the whole time. He will not take his eyes off me; even when he starts to doze off, he rights himself and locks eyes with me again. He is so relaxed in my arms, maybe he is wondering who I am, but he is not afraid. He has not learned fear yet. He is thinking, *Thank you for my bottle, thank you for taking care of me.* And when the bottle is empty, he is asleep.

When I go downstairs, I am a little lighter. I think I will turn babysitting into a thriving business. I will have multiple families who count on me. They will call at the last minute, their voices thick with apologies. "Sorry it's such short notice, Ellie, but we are really in a bind . . . Could you sit for us again tonight?" And I will wave my hand at them, tell them it is nothing. I will need to be careful about double-booking. I will need to buy one of those Filofax things.

Shelley and Rob get home at midnight. I am watching *Friday Night Videos.* They ask how everything went.

"He was an *angel!*" I say, and I wave them off just like I'd pictured doing.

Shelley drives me home. She wants to know the usual stuff, if I like school and if I have a boyfriend. I decide to hold back on the Elvis stuff for now.

"So. Rob and I were thinking? If you weren't busy? Maybe you could sit for Taylor tomorrow night? We might have a party but we're not sure yet?"

This is actually happening. I play it down.

"That would be great." My insides feel like they are doing a little jig. We pull up to my house. It is pitch-black.

"Anyone home?" she says, poking her head around.

"Yes. Sleeping." Our first lie.

She hands me twenty-five dollars. Twenty-five dollars!

"Okay. Well . . . I'll call you tomorrow if we need you to sit. Is that okay?"

"That's fine."

I get out of the car, feel the warm headlights at my back. Try the door. Locked. I walk back to the car.

"I forgot my key." Our second lie. "I don't want to wake anyone. I'm going to go in through the back. Good night!"

The back window is unlocked; I open it, hoist myself over the sill. I did go in through the back, so that was not a lie. I go through the house, open up the front door, wave her off again. Exhale.

I am in bed but cannot sleep. My mind is going for a marathon record. There are little gifts every day. You think you know about everything then, bam, the universe says, *Well what about this?* And you have to admit, *Well, no, I hadn't thought of it. But* thank you.

The next morning I am cleaning the bathroom with Gwen. She is tired; she sneaked in sometime after one o'clock. Our mother came in way after that, so we are being extra quiet for her. I am singing "Suspicious Minds" into the toilet brush, but Gwen is not amused. The phone rings. She sprints for it, then comes back to the bathroom, defeated.

"It's someone named Shelley."

Here we go! It is beginning! I pick up the phone, pause a minute, try for casual yet serious.

"Hello?" I lie back on my bed, cross my ankles.

"Hi, Ellie. It's Shelley? Ummm . . . Just wanted to make sure everything is all right?"

"Everything's fine. How are you?" Silence.

"Um . . . Ellie? Your . . . mother called here last night?" I feel my stomach fall. I am silent, so she continues. "She wanted to know where you were?"

"What?" I stall. "What time?"

"It was three-thirty in the morning." Inside she said *young lady.* I could feel it.

"But I don't understand . . . I was home."

"I see." There is something in her tone. "Ellie? Is your mother there now?"

"Yes."

"May I speak with her then?"

"Well . . . she is sleeping." Not a lie.

"Right. Of course she is."

All at once I know what happened. She came home, too out of it to know any better, and instead of calling for me, or checking my room, she called the number by the phone. I can just hear her sloppy voice breathing into the receiver, completely oblivious to everything. But not.

"Shelley." There is an ache in my voice; there's so much I want to say. I see Taylor's big, trusting eyes. She doesn't let me finish, anyway.

"Ellie. This isn't going to work out. I'm sorry."

She hangs up the phone. I imagine her putting it down with just her thumb and forefinger so as to make sure she didn't get any of me on her, wiping her hands off on her skirt just to be certain.

I stay on my bed, same position, unable to move, embarrassed by all my plans. The pin in the balloon. It is not a sudden pop, but a slow air leak. It whizzes slowly down to the ground, where it arrives empty.

Gwen's voice echoes from the bathroom, "Come *on,* Ellie! This isn't fair! You have to help!"

"Be *quiet!*" My mother screams from behind her bedroom door. I jerk at the sound, then feel my jaw tighten. My cheeks begin to get hot, then they start to throb. I clench my hands into fists, my nails dig into my palms, but the pain is a relief. In my every cell, every fiber of me, is this thought, and it surprises me, but what I think is: *I could kill her and leave here and never speak her name.*

I get up and go to her door. I knock as a warning, then swing the door open. It is so dark in there, but I can make out the shape of her on the bed. On the nightstand are empty bottles. Gin, mostly.

"Mom?" Silence. I look for signs of life, the subtle rise and fall of the sheets. She raises her head, squints at me.

"I can't take you anywhere today, Ellie. Mommy doesn't feel good."

"That," I say, "is because you are hung *over*." My voice startles me, but it does not scare me. It is quite a shocking thing, how rage can build. It sits still in your belly like a stone, then suddenly, with the right invitation, it is banging on your insides demanding to be let out. I grind my teeth so hard my jaw cracks like a knuckle. I fantasize for a moment about how good it would feel to just end it. End her.

"Shut the door now, Ellie. Mommy's tired."

I stand there motionless. In the moment of quiet between rage and action, there is sadness. I look at her on the bed, lumped pathetically in the center. Feel my rage begin to turn into something else. A memory comes to me.

When I was five, my mother took me for a ride on her bike. I felt confined in the baby seat, so she unfastened the seat belt for me and told me to hold on good. About twenty minutes in, she tried to ride up on the curb. But she lost her balance, the bike fell over, and we tumbled onto the road. I started crying. Her voice was kind but shaky. "Oh. It's okay. We're okay. Shush now." She stood up and began to pull the bike off the road, and I began screaming. My foot was caught in the spokes of the wheel, wedged in there good, purple, and not budging. I saw my mother's face when she discovered my foot. I watched the fear settle over her. She ran in every direction, screaming for help. When no one arrived to help, she came and sat beside me and smoothed my hair. Hard. I could see her eyes darting around. When still nobody came, she pulled her knees to her chest, hugged them, and rocked herself back and forth.

Under her breath I could hear her saying, "I don't know what to do. I don't know what to do," over and over.

I remember thinking, "Well, I am *five*." But still, I felt some part of me reach over, relieve her of some of that weight, put it onto me. Even then I knew she wasn't strong enough for all of it. But somehow, I knew *I* was.

I swallow the courage it took to come in here, then begin to back out the door. Before I am gone, she lifts her head from the pillow.

"You're a good girl, Ellie."

"Go back to sleep."

"Ellie? You love me, don't you?"

"Yes, Mommy," I say. "I love you." But one day, I will be gone. And today will be one of the reasons why.

She settles her head on the pillow. I back out of the room and close the door. I lean my head against the frame, allow just a few quiet tears of frustration, then I finish cleaning the bathroom like I am supposed to. But I do not sing again, and I scrub hard at the tub, like there might be gold beneath it. Or freedom. Or kindness.

eight

Well, I am too fat for my bathing suit. It is a brown two-piece and my sides are bulging out around the waist part. I look like a kielbasa whose casing has burst.

"That's not going to work, is it?" Gwen offers her two cents, which, really, she could have saved. Today the pool is opening in our neighborhood. You have to be sixteen to go without an adult, and since Gwen is still grounded, my mother is making her take me.

"My God, Ellie." My mother has now come into my bedroom; she and Gwen are circling me, wondering what to do. The good news is that my breasts have gotten bigger. "You can't go out like that." She is right. It is bordering on obscene. My mother disappears for a moment and returns with a tiny green bathing suit in her hand. It is hers from last year.

"Try this," she says and pushes it at me.

"It's smaller than the one I have on!"

"Try it. It stretches."

She is right. It does. The fabric is puckered or something. Once I am into the suit, a one-piece, things are much better. It is a tank-style suit with a scoop back and high-cut legs. It covers all the worst parts.

Gwen, on the other hand, looks perfect in her black string bikini. Her skin is already a natural golden brown. Her breasts are perfect B cups and the rest of her is all petite and toned like a dancer, which is not fair because she only took ballet for a year when she was six. I always wonder if that was the thing that tipped the scales in her favor, though, that one year of ballet. I never took ballet, so maybe that is why I ended up with this body instead. We were allowed to pick one activity that year and, damn it, I picked horseback riding. Now Gwen looks like a prima ballerina with breasts and I, well, let's just say I fill out a saddle.

"I can't go out like this!" I cry out and throw myself onto my bed in my most dramatic fashion.

"Fine with me," Gwen says. She has been trying to get out of this all day.

"Oh, yes, you are. You are both going." My mother is very anxious to get rid of us. It is Memorial Day weekend and Reggie has the day off. "You look fine. I need you girls out of my hair today. Besides, Ellie, you could use some color."

Well, my holiday is starting off just fine. I am fat, pale, and my sister would rather die than spend the day with me. Gwen gets up and storms into the bathroom. My mother yells at her to not slam the door, but she does anyway. When she is done in there, Gwen comes out and announces that her period has just started and she is definitely not going to the pool. My mother shifts all her weight to her left side, puts her hand on her hip, and says that as a woman you cannot allow your period to run your life. For a minute I am excited by all this intimate talk. This girl talk about periods and so forth. I am newly initiated. I only got my period last fall. I am still waiting for all of our periods to synch up, so that we get them at the same time like I have heard happens. That happens with Celia and her mom. A couple days before they get it, Mrs. Meyers buys them a big tub of ice cream and they eat it right out of the carton with extra-big spoons. Celia says her mom craves chocolate ice cream especially. That is another thing I am looking forward to: PMS. So far, my appetite is the same as before my period comes.

When I finally got my period, I was at school of all places. I went to the bathroom and peed just like every other day, but when I got up to flush, there was blood in the water. At first I was scared, and I made the girl in the next stall go to the Art hall and find Gwen. When Gwen got there, she just laughed and said I'd gotten the curse, and she gave me a pad to wear. I remember I was really excited the whole rest of the day. I was thinking that now I, Gwen, and my mom would have something in common. On the way to the store my mom would stop and say, "Hey, Ellie, do we need tampons?" because I would know if we were low on them. I couldn't wait to tell my mother and to be pressed into the bosom of womanhood.

Needless to say, things did not go as planned. When she got home from work that night, I greeted her at the top of the stairs and Gwen said, "Ellie got her period today!" I stood there and mocked embarrassment, even though inside I felt utterly triumphant. But my mother didn't say anything. Instead her eyes welled up and she said, in a voice barely audible, "Call your father." *Call your father?* She walked into the kitchen and picked up the phone, dialed.

When my dad answered she said, not hello, but, "Your daughter has something to tell you," and she handed me the phone. Then she stood there and watched me as I searched for the words. I was thinking how odd it was that I had gotten my period and now I was trying to tell my dad. Somehow my mother had made it about him. I watched her in the doorway with her arms crossed, hanging on my every word, her lips pursed so tightly the outside edges were white, and I realized: For my mother, it is always about him. Everything, every day, says *He left you.* Even this.

Gwen says, "I can't go to the pool while I'm on the rag! It's gross!" My mother tells her not to be so dramatic. But Gwen continues. I sit down on my bed, watch my milky thighs spread out, wait for the scene to crescendo.

"I am goddamn *not* going! This is *bull*shit!"

My mother's face clinches up tight, reddens. "Gwenevere. Would it kill you. To do something nice. For your sister." She is containing it all, keeping it at a simmer. "Just once. That is all. I am asking."

Gwen seems annoyed by her inability to provoke our mother. That is usually how she gets out of it. A big, horrible scene ensues and Gwen gets to storm out. All of those confrontations between them, and at the end of the day, it is really just Gwen's way of avoiding. You'd think she'd find another way.

Gwen turns her eyes to me. "Are you happy? You big baby!"

I am stunned quiet. I'm not used to having her venom directed at me. It is so mortifying that I am not old enough to go to the pool alone. That is a very stupid rule.

"Don't you start in with Ellie now!" My mother actually rescues me. "Please just do this, Gwen. Go get your flip-flops." When Gwen goes for her shoes, my mother goes into her bedroom and gets out her pink sarong with the fringe. She knows I love it. She says, "You can borrow this today," and gives me a little smile from the corner of her mouth and winks at me. I just stare back, grateful. Today I am her favorite. I touch my arms, the comforter on my bed, try to anchor myself in the moment, so that maybe I can remember this during the other times.

When Gwen and I finally get to the pool, it is adult-swim only, so all the little kids are running urgently around the perimeter waiting for the fifteen minutes to be up. We find two lounge chairs by the lifeguard chair and lay our towels down. I love the way the sun feels on my skin, like it is baking me. It rides up just to the line of being too hot, of burning, but never crosses it. The air smells like chlorine and concrete.

In the pool at the deep end is a girl in a hot-pink bikini with silver studs on the top. Her hair is Sun-In blond and she is nervously twirling a strand of it around her finger. She has pink lipstick on (in the pool!) that matches her bikini. She is talking to a guy; his back is to us. Her giggle carries down to where we are sunbathing, and Gwen sighs and slides her eyes upward. Just then there is a very loud whistle blown. The lifeguard yells, "All-swim!" and there is a cacophony of squeals and splashes as the kids hurl themselves back into the pool.

The girl in the pink bikini uses the ladder in the deep end to hoist herself out of the pool. You can tell that she is worried the kids will get her hair wet. The guy she was talking to swims a lap before getting out, and when he does, I see that it is Leo. His skin is brown and shiny and he is wearing cut-off jeans for a bathing suit.

He makes a water trail right past us as he goes over to a lounge chair. Gwen sits up and takes notice of him as he lays his towel out. Then she speaks her first words to me all day.

"Who," she says, "is that *fox*?" She sits up and poses on the lounge chair, pulls her shades down to the edge of her nose to get a better look.

"That's Leo," I say, suddenly aware that she looks like the Bain de Soleil model in her black bikini, and I look like the girl in the Noxzema commercial who forgot to wear enough sunscreen.

"How do *you* know?" She props herself up on her elbows.

"Because I talked to him."

"You did *not*."

I sit up in my lounge chair and look over to where Leo is lying, scanning first for Pink-Bikini Chick.

"Hi, Leo!" I say and wave big. Startled, he looks up.

"Hey, Ellie." He nods in acknowledgment. I settle back into my lounge chair, resist the urge to stick my tongue out at Gwen.

"So," she says, completely unimpressed, "what do you know about him?"

"All I know is, he's staying with his parents for a while, and he doesn't seem too happy about it."

"Yeah well, who *is*?"

It is an hour later and I think I have gotten too much sun. When I press on my leg, my finger leaves a white mark that lasts a very long time. I tell Gwen I think we should go. She gathers our things and makes sure we walk right past Leo on our way out. I check to make sure my sarong is covering everything.

"Good-bye, Leo."

He rolls up onto his elbows. "See ya."

On the way home, we take our flip-flops off and have a contest to see who can walk on the blacktop longest. Gwen does an exaggerated chicken walk.

"Hey, if Mom's in a good mood, maybe she'll take us to High's for ice cream. I call Mint Chocolate Chip! You can't get the same as me."

"Don't worry," I say. "I'm never eating again."

We finally hit the grass, our feet burning.

"Woulda been a tie," she says, " but extra points for originality means I win."

• • •

When we get home and walk in the door, something immediately feels wrong. I go into the kitchen and see a chair knocked over. The refrigerator door has been left open too.

Gwen calls out, "Mom?" But there is no answer.

We go upstairs and knock on her door. No answer. Gwen opens it. But the room is empty. In her bathroom, we see a light on.

"Mommy? Are you in there?" Gwen knocks on the bathroom door. We hear the slightest sound of water sloshing around, but no reply. Gwen opens the door. My mother is in the bathtub, her head is cocked back, she is barely conscious. Balancing on the ledge of the tub is the cordless telephone and a glass of gin with little pebbles of half-melted ice cubes. My mother raises her head; her eye makeup has run down to the corners of her mouth. She can't seem to right herself. Every time she lifts her head up, it falls back down, forward and backward, like her neck muscles have given out. She is smashed like I have never seen. She blindly reaches out for her glass, nearly knocking the phone into the tub with her. Gwen instinctively jumps forward, grabs the phone, and throws it into the bedroom.

My mother knocks back the rest of the gin, then drops the glass in the water. It bobs on the surface as she slides down into the tub and her head goes underwater. Gwen reaches over and pulls her up by her underarms, but when she lets go, our mother slides right back under.

"Ellie! Help me!"

I go over to help, but it is awkward with us both reaching over trying to hold our mother up, so I am kind of just in the way.

"We have to get her out of here! Help me pull her out!"

On three, we pull her by her arms over the side of the tub. When half of her is out, Gwen steps into the bathtub and hoists our mother's legs over the side too. We try to lift her crumpled body off the floor but can't. We end up dragging her onto the carpet in her bedroom. Gwen starts patting our mother's face, hard-like, to wake her up. Finally she lifts her head up, makes a groggy, unintelligible sound, and crawls the rest of the way to her bed.

I pull the covers over her naked little body. I see the scar on her belly from where I came out of her. It is just above where her hairline starts. She is blond down there.

"Mom? Where's Reggie?" Gwen asks her. Then our mother starts crying. It's that loud, ugly crying too, not the pretty strolling tears.

"Gone," she says. She says it over and over. Gone, gone, gone. Gone. Like a song. Then, "Leave me alone!" She flails a hand in our direction.

Gwen shakes her head and goes over to the window to pull the shade down. I concur by saying, "Good idea. Let her sleep it off."

"Will you girls shut the hell up?" It is a relief that she is able to yell, so I say to Gwen, "Let's leave her alone now. We can keep checking on her."

The thing with my mother is that I feel like I am always waiting to see what I will get from her, kindness or cruelty. Usually it is the latter, and maybe it is only because of that kernel of kindness from earlier, but this time her words nearly break me in half.

"Listen to Miss Piggy," she says. "She knows *everything.*" We head for the door, but she is not finished with me.

"Take off my bathing suit before you ruin it! And you better go buy some bread before I wake up. You little oinker! I know what you did." She tries to make a snorting sound, but she chokes on it and ends up coughing instead.

"Oh, that's real nice, Mom," Gwen says. "We just saved your life."

"You ruined my life." She starts to cry, for real this time, from a lonely place I don't get to see. "I was beautiful." I see Gwen wipe away a tear and choke back whatever else wants to come. Then my mother sits up, and with that voice we know well she says, "You hear me? You girls *ruined* me!"

Gwen starts crying now. Then, her voice flat, she says, "We should have let you drown." Then she takes my hand and leads me out the door, closing it behind us.

In the hall, Gwen avoids looking at me. She just says, "Give me the bathing suit. I'll do a load of wash."

I go into my room and change my clothes. Gwen comes in, without knocking of course, and hands me two one-dollar bills.

"You should go get bread" is all she says.

• • •

By the time I am walking back from the store, it is nearly dark. It is around seven o'clock but it is Daylight Saving Time so the sun gets to hang on just a while longer. I can't think of anything that I love as much as Daylight Saving Time. Not even Christmas.

When I am nearly home, I see Leo come out of his house. He is wearing tight black jeans, a black T-shirt, and a pair of bulky motorcycle boots. He sees me as he is walking to his van.

"Hi, Leo."

He passes his van and walks over to me. "You got some sun, huh?"

"Yeah. Too much." Not only do I look like a lobster but my shins are already starting to blister.

"Man, that looks like it hurts. Does it hurt?"

"A little."

"You should put something on that."

"Like what?"

"Got any benzocain?"

I've never heard of it, but I'm assuming the answer is no. I shake my head.

"Come inside."

I follow him into his house, stopping in the foyer.

"Wait here."

He heads down the hall and disappears into the powder room. His house is the same layout as ours, but reversed.

I peek my head around the corner into the kitchen. I can't believe the wallpaper in there. It is a dark burgundy floral with bunches of enormous cabbage roses scattered across it. It is much too busy for a room this size, and the subject matter is inappropriate for a kitchen. If there were fruit on there instead, that would be more fitting. But still, the color is suffocating. If it were our kitchen, mine and Leo's, I'd like it to be light colors. Like maybe a warm ivory or a cheerful butter yellow. Yellow is a color that creates a feeling of happiness. I bet that if you are happy while you cook, the food tastes better.

Leo emerges from the bathroom holding a little aerosol can with a blue cap.

"Gimme your leg."

I hold up my leg and he sprays each shin, one at a time. The stuff is white and smells like a doctor's office, but it feels like someone put out the fire.

He hands me the can. "Take it," he says. "You're gonna need it."

"Thank you."

"Sure."

We walk back outside. He gets into his van and starts the engine, rolls his window down.

"Where are you going?" I ask.

"Band practice."

The music blares from inside as he drives off. Finally I go back inside and put the bread on the counter, take the aerosol can to my bedroom.

At eleven o'clock the phone rings. I hear my mother answer, then, after a minute or so, I think I hear her *laughing*.

Before I started school, I was home all day with my mother. After we were done with chores, we would watch soap operas, and then we'd color in my coloring books. She was hands down the world's best colorer. All of her crayon marks went in the same direction and blended together beautifully. Plus, she always stayed in the lines. A feat I could never master. I liked to embellish my pictures by drawing hearts and stars around the border. Only, my stars were more like two triangles, one on top of the other, pointing in opposite directions, or what I now know is the Star of David. I was frustrated because I wanted to make big-girl stars like Gwen could make.

At my request, my mother sprawled out beside me on the floor, propped herself on her elbows, and got to work. First she tried explaining that it was one continuous line and I didn't have to lift my crayon off the paper to make a star. When I didn't get it, she drew a few stars on the paper and let me trace them. With her hand over mine we counted, "One, two, three, four, five," until the blue crayon star on top perfectly matched her yellow crayon star underneath. Between you and me, I saw the pattern before I even started tracing her stars. But she was sitting so close to me, her long, blond hair in waves tickling my face, speaking in that high, soft voice. Being so patient with me. *Try again, Ellie. One, two, three, four . . .* Well, I could have sat there forever.

Sometimes I think it is okay that my mother doesn't love me anymore, because she did. And I remember. I only wish I had known it would stop. I would have paid better attention, saved up everything in reserves like when they thought the bomb was coming. But I hadn't known. I just hadn't known.

nine

I am in history class. Mr. Finkle has invited a follower of the B'hai religion to come and speak. It is for this thing called SAS day. It stands for Sensitivity Awareness Symposium, and what happens is, once a year during sixth period someone from a different culture or religion comes and talks about what it is like to be different, and we are all supposed to feel enlightened and better about ourselves for listening. So I'm sitting here all period while a devout follower of B'hai stands before me and tells us that our purpose in this world is to develop wisdom, to love, and to advance spiritually, and all I can think about is how much better my life would be if my thighs were thinner.

I pass a note to Celia. It says:

C,
Only 10 days until the last day of school. We register

*for next year on the 18th. Exams are on the 15th and
16th. So as far as real school days are concerned we
only have 7 left. 10 if you include exams and registra-
tion. 12 if you count weekends.*

I am suddenly good at math. Celia reads my note, jots down
her response, and passes it to me. All of this was done without
her taking her eyes off our B'hai speaker. Her note says,

> *E,*
>
> *Your math abilities are highly selective. One thing you
> didn't mention: It is only 13 days until I leave for
> camp!*

Apparently my memory is highly selective, as well. I have
chosen to forget that Celia will be going to camp for the summer. She's gone every year since she was nine, and this year
she is very excited because she will get to be a counselor-in-
training. A CIT, as she calls it. I am going with her to buy supplies after school, then I'm sleeping over. It's all been arranged.
After seventh period I am meeting her out front and we are taking the bus to her house.

Later that night, we have gone to Kmart for supplies, drained
her shampoo and conditioner into smaller plastic bottles, and
written her name on everything plastic with a glittery purple
pen. We have had dinner (lasagna and salad, with ice cream
for dessert), so all that is left now is sleeping. But, of course,

we can't. When I stay over at her house we get to sleep in the guest room, which has two twin beds. We lie on our sides, facing each other, each propped up by one elbow, and talk till our throats hurt. Her parents are right next door and they never tell us to get to bed or keep it down. When there is a lull in the conversation, we lie on our backs and listen to the air conditioner. Then, eventually, there is a voice in the dark.

"Ellie?"

"Hmmm?"

"Do you think I should go all the way with Kevin?"

This is a big question, and not one I take lightly. I weigh my words carefully before forming them.

"No. I do not."

"Why?"

The truth is, I don't know why. First, like me, she is only fourteen.

"I *am* almost fifteen, Ellie."

I should have been more careful, because now she is defensive. But I don't know of any reason why she shouldn't, other than if she did, it would be something else she had that I didn't. And that is ugly of me.

"You haven't known him long enough."

"We've been together almost a month!"

"But you're *leaving.*"

"That's why I want to!"

"That's exactly why you shouldn't."

"I don't follow."

"Because as soon as you get to camp, you will meet someone else and . . ."

"I'll never meet anyone like Kevin!"

"Celia. That's what you always say. If there is one thing I know, it's that you will find another boyfriend at camp. The first day, probably."

Celia is quiet for a minute. But I can hear her mind working.

"You think?" she says finally.

"I *know.*"

She sits up in her bed, puts her pillow in her lap. "What about you?"

"What about me?" I say flatly.

"Do you ever think about it?"

"About what?"

She throws her hands up in exasperation, which was what I was shooting for.

"About doing it!"

"Who would I do it with? I mean, come on. You know my track record."

"Seriously. You'd have to go dig someone up."

"Eeeewww! You are so gross!" I throw my pillow at her. She stacks it happily on top of the other one. Now I have no pillow, so I sit up and scrunch up the comforter into my lap. It's more comfortable with something in your lap, and for some reason it seems to make talking easier.

"Really, though, Ellie. If you only like dead guys, how are you ever going to have sex?"

She has a point. And the first thing that comes to mind is

Leo. But it is too new. I'm afraid that if I say anything, he'll evaporate. But I can't resist.

"Well," I say. Celia sits up at full attention. It is delicious. "There is this guy."

"What *guy*?" Her tone is more suspicious than anything.

"Well," I say again, and she is getting irritated so I hurry. "I don't know much about him. He lives across the street."

"Across the street! Alive *and* geographically desirable? This is good. What else?"

"Like I said, I don't know much about him. We've only talked a couple of times. His parents live across the street and he's visiting them for a while or something. Oh! And he gave me the stuff for my sunburn."

"Oh, my God! He likes you!"

"No way!" But my heart does a mini-Charleston.

"That's what boys do when they like you, they give you things. What else? What else do you know? How old is he? What's he look like?"

"Well, he's *very* cute. *Tall.* Dark hair, brown eyes . . ."

"*Really?* What else? How old is he?"

"Well, last time I saw him he said something about band practice, so I'm guessing he's a musician or something. I don't know how old he is. Maybe twenty."

"*Twenty?*"

"So?"

"A *musician*?" Celia throws herself backward onto the bed.

"What's the problem? I thought he was geographically desirable."

"It's out of the question!"

"Why?" I feel like something is being taken from me that I didn't even know I had in the first place. "Why is it out of the question?"

"Ellie. First of all, you are fourteen. No twenty-year-old guy is gonna like a fourteen-year-old girl. It's not even legal!"

"Uh, *hello*? Elvis was twenty-*four* when he met Priscilla."

"Plus, he's a musician! He's got groupies!"

"How do you know?"

"They all do. My dad was a trumpet player in the army. I know how that works." This is all way too much. I want to yell at her. Tell her to shut up because she knows nothing and her life is perfect so she should mind her own business. But I am at her house and it is two A.M. So instead I say, "You're probably right. I just thought he was cute."

She is not finished. "Well, you should really try to like someone, you know, more *obtainable*. Like Arnie. Why won't you go out with him? He thinks you're really cute."

"I don't know, *Celia*." I try to hide my irritation, but it seeps out between my teeth. "I'm just not interested in him."

"*Why?* He's totally adorable. Those big blue eyes! Any girl at school would die to go out with him in a second."

"Well, what can I say? He just doesn't do it for me."

Celia's tone changes. "Ellie," she says, "the only reason you don't like Arnie is because he likes *you*. You only want what you can't have. You're not interested in anybody available."

I consider this for a moment. "I don't think that's it."

"No?"

"No. Someone like Arnie, I don't know, there's no *spark*. His light just isn't bright enough. Do you know what I mean? Take Elvis for example. Now *there* was someone with light. You were just drawn to it, you could warm yourself just by standing next to him. Someone with an energy and a light that strong. It's . . . *intoxicating*. That's what I want. That's what I'm looking for. Not *Arnie*."

"Look, I don't know what that's supposed to mean. All I'm saying is, I just wish you'd get a boyfriend and have some fun for once."

I am tired and not up for fighting, so I let her have the last word this time. I lie back down and turn off my light. But in my head, in the dark, I see Leo. His hair held back by his sunglasses and that smile meant just for me. I pull him closer to me, closer than I'd let myself before, and for a moment I allow the possibility.

The next day, I am at school, in third period, counting the number of punched-out paper circles on the carpet, when I look up and see my guidance counselor, Mr. Harmon, come into the classroom. He looks exactly like Orville Redenbacher, the popcorn guy. He whispers something to my teacher, who nods and calls me over.

"Ellie? Mr. Harmon would like to see you." There is a hurried whisper among the rest of the class. I look around the room with just my eyes then walk quickly up to the front.

"What's wrong?" I ask. But he won't answer me. He just says I need to come with him to the office. The whole way there I am running over in my mind what I possibly could have done. When we finally get to his office, I see that it is full. The principal is there, a small, mousy lady I don't know, and a police officer.

"Have a seat, please." Mr. Harmon says, so I do.

"Is my mother dead?"

Everyone looks uncomfortably at each other, then Mr. Harmon begins waving his arms, "No. No, no, no. Everything's fine. Okay? We just need to ask you some questions."

The principal, Mr. Cole, begins to speak. He is a big man with dark skin and thinning hair. There are little black strands raked across the top of his head from all sides. He got transferred here from North Carolina, and he looks like an old Southern gentleman, minus the seersucker suit, cane, and mint julep.

"Ellie," he says, "where were you last night?"

"I stayed the night at Celia's." My answer is automatic; I didn't stop to wonder why he was asking.

"Who?"

"Celia Meyers."

"I see." He tilts his glasses down to look at me. "Would Mr. or Mrs. Meyers be able to verify that?"

"Yes, sir."

"I see." He nods to the mousy lady, who gets up and leaves. Mr. Cole leans in to me a little. "Do you know where Gwen was last night?"

"Gwen? No, sir. I don't." Mr. Cole frowns, deepening the wrinkles in his forehead.

"I see." Which sounds benign but also like there is another meaning behind it.

"What is going on?" I say. "Where is Gwen?" Mr. Harmon scoots his chair closer to mine. He's being very gentle.

"Ellie," he says, "we don't know where Gwen is. She is not in school today. But we got a call saying that she was seen with some other kids, known associates of hers, down at the old mill house last night."

"Oh. Well, I wouldn't know."

Mr. Cole sighs heavily and shifts in his chair. "Do Gwen and her associates ever go there? Do they trespass there?"

"Lots of kids do."

"Do *you*?"

"No, sir."

"You've never been there?"

I stare at the floor and feel the sweat rush to my palms. Images of the old mill flash into my mind; I try to shake them out.

"No," I say again. "I have never been there."

Mr. Harmon is now playing the good-guy role in the good cop/bad cop routine, while the actual cop just stands there, stone-faced. "Ellie. It is very important that we find Gwen."

"I understand. But I don't know where she is. I was at Celia's. Besides, Gwen is grounded, so I'm sure she wasn't there."

"Well, we've tried to call your mother and we can't get ahold of her."

"What is this really about?" I ask finally.

Mr. Harmon looks at the ground, then at the other men in the room. He avoids my eyes. "Ellie, the old mill house burned down last night. Officer Reinholdt is here to arrest your sister."

I feel the burn deep in my stomach, instinctively grab onto the chair arms.

"I see." It's all I can say.

"Ellie. You must understand that if you help her, you are aiding and abetting. You are breaking the law."

You are breaking the law. The words are too heavy for me to hold them. I do not know anything except that deep down in me is a thought that won't go away: *I know it was her who did this.*

I look down at the speckled squares of tile, then back up at the wall. Above Mr. Cole's head is a blue and orange pennant: *Go Cougars! State Champs 1987.*

"I don't know anything," I say quietly. "I don't know anything at all."

The men inhale simultaneously, and Mr. Cole's chair scrapes against the floor as he backs it away from his desk. "Very well, then," he says. "You should go back to class." He scratches out a hall pass and hands it to me. Like I can really concentrate on Government at a time like this. Before I walk out the door, he says, "If you see your sister, it is imperative that you tell this office. There will be consequences if you don't."

When I get to History class, Celia sneaks in just as the bell is ringing. She is flustered as she rushes to her seat. She immediately tears out a page from her notebook and scribbles a note to me. When Mr. Finkle turns his back to write on the chalkboard, she passes it to me with urgent eyes. I open it quietly under my desk. It says, *My mom won't let me go to Kevin's basketball game tonight and now he's mad at me. Help!*

I look over at her, slouched back in her chair with her arms crossed. I close up the note and tuck it into my history folder. I am thinking that, when God started handing out problems, he knew what he was doing. There is no way on earth Celia could be me.

A few months ago they started making blue M&Ms in addition to the usual colors. Every day at lunch, for *weeks,* I'd watch Celia fish M&Ms out of the bag, inevitably retrieve a blue one, and rear her head in exasperation. "I *just* can't get *used* to the *blue* ones!" It became a spectator sport for me, watching her pull out a blue M&M and waiting for her world to tip on its axis. "Give it to me," I'd say. "I'll eat it."

We walk to seventh period together, but I don't tell her about Gwen. When I get to my seat in Study Hall, it is the same thing all over again, only this time with Greg. He rushes in at the bell, sits down, and writes a note. He passes it to me and I take it from him dutifully. Fully expecting to read about his good problem, I unfold the note.

It says, *Is it true about Gwen?*

I feel my heart jump at the words. I crumple up the note and shake my head to say I don't know. He writes on another piece of paper and hands it to me.

Where is she?

Again I shake my head. Greg starts to write another note, and I reach over and grab his hand.

"Why do you care so much?" I ask. He just shrugs his shoulders. "You don't still like her, do you?"

Greg's eyes dart to the floor and he picks at his thumb. "I think she's really pretty," he says. The study hall monitor gives me the no-talking glare.

"We'll talk after class," I say. Then I pick up *To Kill a Mockingbird,* which we already read in English class back in January but I am reading again because I began to miss everyone in the story so much. I will not look up from my book until the bell rings.

I am trying to concentrate, trying to lose myself in the world of Scout and Atticus. I think I love Calpernia as much as Scout does. But I barely get through a paragraph without the old mill house flashing in front of the page. I see the old pieces of glowing wood falling away from the frame. And I see Gwen standing off to the side, calmly, blowing her smoke rings.

When the bell rings, Greg stands up and looks at me.

"Well?" he says expectantly, like it's all going to come pouring out of me.

"Well, nothing."

"You said we'd talk after class."

"I don't know what's going on."

"You can tell me. I won't say anything to anyone."

"Greg, she doesn't even know you exist."

He stares at me blankly for a second, then looks away. "I know," he says. "I wasn't . . . I just thought maybe I could help." He gathers his books. "You need a ride home?"

I hate guilt. It is so useless. You just sit there feeling bad about something you've already done. And in real life there are no take-backs. You can try a do-over, but the whole thing is tainted already.

"I'm sorry. This is just . . . a lot. You know?"

"Yeah," he says, then points at my desk with his chin. "Get your stuff. Let's get out of here."

On the way home Greg says he has to stop at Safeway. He told his mom he would get hamburger buns. I love this grocery store, especially the bakery section. Sometimes the lady behind the counter breaks up cookies and puts them on a plate for customers to sample. She's really nice for thinking of doing that, and also because I always make more than one trip and she never says anything about it. She just smiles and says, "They're good, huh?" which shows she takes pride in her work, since she baked them herself.

When we pull into the Safeway lot, Greg says I don't have to come in because he will just be a second. But I say, "Oh, no, I'll come in with you," because I am thinking about the cookie lady.

As we are walking into the store I hear, well, *sounds* coming from the bushes just off to the side. I look over. It's Gwen. She is crouched behind the bushes at Safeway.

"*Psst.*" She actually says that.

I go over to where she is. She motions for me to come closer. As in, she wants me to crouch behind the bushes at Safeway *also*. Greg has noticed that I am not behind him and comes over to the bushes.

"It's Gwen!" he announces so everyone in the town can hear.

We are a chorus of *Ssshhhhh!* Then a hand reaches up and yanks Greg behind the bushes. It appears that Justina Simpson is back there as well. Suddenly it is a party, and I am the one with my nose pressed to the window. Reluctantly, I hoist myself over the bushes too.

"Hey, girl!" Gwen says and hugs me. She is a fugitive, and having the time of her life.

"Jesus," I say, as the mulch digs into my knees. "What are you doing here?"

"Looking for you. We were making our way toward school."

"Gwen, if they see you, they'll arrest you."

"I know. You gotta help us."

"You have to turn yourself in."

Justina snarls at me. "See? I told you she'd say that."

"Ellie. I can't."

"They just want to talk to you. You didn't do it, right?" Gwen and Justina exchange a look. Gwen nods. It is a small nod, but there is no hiding her satisfaction. "Oh, God."

Greg covers his ears. "I didn't hear that." Gwen turns to him.

"Dude. It was *crazy.* It just got so out of hand!"

Justina does her snickery stoner laugh. "Listen," she says, "we're going to need a place to stay."

Gwen nods. "We were at Putt-Putt this morning, but they kicked us out."

"We had to wait in the freakin' woods all day. It sucked." Justina turns to Greg. "Dude, can you hook us up?"

Greg's eyes widen. I can see he wants to run, but his eyes meet with Gwen's and I see the thought walk into his head.

"Um, you could probably hang out in my garage." Gwen smiles at him. Justina sneers. "It's not like a *normal* garage," he assures her. "My brother stays there when he's home from college. It's really nice."

Justina does her usual thing of acting like everyone around her is the lamest person on earth, then she says, "Dude, that is never gonna work."

"Why not?"

"Think about it, Sherlock. First of all, where are your parents? Aren't they gonna know if we're in your *garage,* for God's sake?"

Greg looks over at Gwen. Her eyebrows are raised in waiting.

"Well," he stammers. "Not necessarily."

"Whatever, dude." Justina waves him off.

"No. Wait. Seriously. If you keep the lights off and keep quiet, they'll never know." Gwen looks at Justina, now in charge, and searches her face. "I'll bring you guys food later. It'll be cool, I promise."

Justina eyes him up and down. "Why are you doing this?" she asks him. Greg looks at me, then back to the ground. Justina puts her face closer to his. "You got a hard-on for me?" Greg's face goes white; I hear him swallow. Justina breaks out in laughter. She slaps him on the shoulder and points at him. "You shoulda seen your face!"

Greg takes a deep breath. Gwen rubs his forearm. "That's really cool of you," she says.

"Okay," Justina says. "We'll just hang out there until the heat dies down. Then we'll get out of your hair."

Greg arranges to pick them up behind the building so as not to risk being seen. He is acting like he is suddenly an expert at covert operations. But what is more true is that Greg is like someone at the zoo who's come to see all the exotic creatures and their behavior, to peek in on a world that is different from his, one that prior to this moment he has only seen on TV.

Greg and I get back into the car, hamburger buns be damned, and pull around to the back of the building. We wait for a minute but don't see any sign of Gwen or Justina. Then, all of a sudden, they bolt out from behind a Dumpster and jump into the car. They throw themselves down on the seat and Greg actually squeals his wheels as he drives away. I can feel my pulse in my throat.

After about a minute, there is a voice from the backseat.

"Turn up the tunes, man!" And he does. We drive to Greg's house, not in terrified silence or in heavy discussion about what is to come, but listening to Metallica on full blast, while Justina and Gwen rock out on the backseat as though they hadn't a care in the world. Then there is me in the front seat, wringing my hands.

When we were kids, our father took Gwen and me to an amusement park. On every ride, Gwen reacted wildly. She kicked and screamed, threw herself onto the floor of the compartment, and at one point, her arms thrashing wildly, she actually knocked our father's front tooth loose. She was unable to contain all that was going on inside her, her mixture of terror and exhilaration, yet at the same time she wanted to ride again and again and again. My reaction was considerably different. I held on tight and didn't make a sound. And at the worst part, when the roller coaster would make the steep climb before the free fall, I simply held on tighter and closed my eyes. It was not in denial of what was happening. I simply knew that if I kept it together, it would all be over soon enough.

After Greg gets the girls situated in his garage, he drops me off at home. When I get inside the house, it is approximately seven hundred degrees in there. Another thing my mother hates besides messiness is air conditioning. We have it but are not allowed to use it. When it gets this hot, Gwen will usually turn it on after school, then turn it off about an hour before our mom gets home. As you may have guessed, I do not have Gwen's courage, so instead I decide to do my homework on the grass under the walnut tree that's next to our house.

I am deep in algebra when I see Leo come out from his house. The truth is, I had this planned in my head. I even put on lip gloss just in case. He's coming over. I casually look up from my algebra book and flutter a wave off the tips of my fingers, then look back to my book! My insides are looking at each other like I am nuts.

"Hi."

"Hi." I close my book now. Smile big. Too big, I guess, because my top lip starts to twitch. I adjust it slightly. He stands over me, blocking the sun from my face.

"Is that your homework?" He takes a cigarette out from behind his ear, rolls it between his fingers.

"Math."

"Yuck."

"Totally."

"Let me see." He returns the cigarette to his ear and squats down beside me. He glances over the page and nods his head. "Pythagoras and I never really got along," he says.

He gathers up a handful of grass and pulls it out of the ground. I have never seen longer eyelashes. He squints up at me.

"Your sunburn's better."

"Oh. Yes. It is. Thank you. For the stuff, I mean."

He nods his head. "So what do you like?"

"Sorry?"

"In school. What subject do you like?"

"Oh. Well, I guess I like English best."

"Yeah? Why is that?"

"I like the words, I guess. Just all the different ways there are to say things. The books just feel so . . . private. Like a conversation between you and the writer."

"*Intimate,* you mean. Like a secret."

I feel the red rush to my face. I avoid his eyes while I nod my head yes.

"So is that what you want to be when you grow up? A writer?"

I feel some part of me soften. It is like the shell that is around my insides has cracked open a little. It is both terrifying and a relief. I realize too that not only do I not have an answer, no one has ever asked me that question. Before I know what to do, I feel tears welling up from deep inside of me, pain from a place

I didn't even know was there. But there is also the paralyzing fear that I will fall apart, and I feel the vigilance in me, that part that keeps me together, come to the rescue, making a little joke to create some distance.

"Actually," I say, "I think I'd like to be a professional video-game player. I *smoke* on Ms. Pac-Man."

Leo smiles, but there is disappointment on his face too.

"Well," he says, "you've got lots of time to think about it." He looks away and pulls some more grass from the ground, then splits a blade in half with his fingers.

"That's not true," I say.

He looks at me. "What? You mean you're not good at Ms. Pac-Man?" He smiles and nudges me slightly with his elbow.

I smile too, then I look at the grass and say quietly, "No. I mean about the writing. I've just . . . I've never told anyone that before."

I see him nod his head. "Okay," he says.

Just then I hear my mother's car turn around the corner. I automatically sit up straighter. She pulls into her parking space, just a few yards or so from where we are sitting. She gets out of the car and is walking toward our door when she notices me sitting there.

"Why are you out here?"

"It's too hot inside." I smile nervously at Leo. *Please, not here, not now.*

"Did you do your chores?"

"I'm doing my homework."

"Well," she says, and looks right at Leo, "it doesn't look like it to me." He coughs uncomfortably.

"I better let you get back to it." He stands up and brushes the grass off his pants, gives a wave to my mother, and walks off. He gets in his van and drives away.

My mother goes into the house and slams the door behind her.

When we had our dog, I used to tie him up to this walnut tree when I gave him a bath. He stood still for me when I had to rub the shampoo in; I guess it felt good. But when it came time to hose him off he would tear into a full-speed run. He'd only get about ten feet before the rope would yank him back, but he wouldn't stop doing it. He didn't seem to care that the rope was around his neck, he just wanted to run. One day he got away and never came back. Gwen was heartbroken. We put up signs, but no one ever called. I was sad he was gone too, but I like to think that he ended up somewhere with sweeping fields, where he has birds to chase, and I imagine that the wind pins his long ears behind him when he runs. I like to think that he has found a good place in the world, one that fits him better than this place did. Sometimes, if I really get to thinking about it, I wonder if that is what my father has done too.

ten

At nine o'clock I am lying in bed when the phone rings.

"Hello?"

"Ellie? It's Greg."

"Is everything okay?"

"A detective just came to my house."

"Oh, God. Where are they?"

"I didn't say anything, I swear. He said someone saw us leaving the Safeway."

"Shit."

I hear someone pick up the phone. "Hello?"

"Mom, hang up!"

"Greg, don't you speak to me like that. You are in for it, young man. Who is this? Who is on the phone?"

"It's Ellie, Mrs. Tucci."

Greg tells me that he's sorry, then his mother tells him to

hang up. "Ellie," she says. "Is your mother there?"

"Yes, ma'am." My God, how my stomach just bungee-jumped.

I call for my mother and hear her pick up the receiver in her bedroom. I tiptoe to her door to see if I can hear anything. I just hear my mother say, "Is that right?" "Uh-huh," and "I'll be right over." I scurry back to my room.

She comes out into the hall but doesn't say a word to me. She is fuming, mumbling under her breath and gathering her keys.

If there is one thing I know, it is this: If my mother has to get out of bed to come get you, you are in the biggest trouble of your life.

They are arguing as they come in the front door.

"That is *it*," my mother says. "Let them take you away. Let's see how you like it in jail!"

"You are a witch! What kind of mother *are* you?"

"The kind that has had it! Get up to your room!"

I hear Gwen stomp up the stairs and slam her door. After an acceptable period of time, I go over and open it slowly. She is listening to her Walkman; she clicks it off, looks at me.

"What do you want?"

"What happened?"

"She's a bitch. She's turning me in."

"Does she know you did it?"

"Of course she does. You told her I did it."

"No, I didn't!"

"Liar."

"But I didn't! She didn't even . . . we didn't even talk about it. I swear to God."

But there is a certain amount of resignation in Gwen. She just shakes her head and shrugs it off. I come over and sit beside her.

"Did Greg tell his mom?"

"He says he didn't. But he totally caved. His mom came into the garage after the cops were there."

"What's going to happen to you?"

"I don't know. I don't care."

I start crying. Gwen tells me to stop. I nod my head up and down over and over, wipe my face with her pillow. "Do you mind?" she says. "That's gross."

"Sorry." I flip the pillow over so the wet marks don't show. "Are they going to take you to jail?"

"How the fuck should I know? I guess so." I begin crying again. I try to keep it small, but it really wants to come.

"Come on, Ellie," she says, pushing me away slightly. But I can't stop. My tears come harder. "Why?" I say, my voice trembling as I try to suck in quick gulps of air. "Why? Why did you do it?"

"I don't know," she says. "I don't know." Then she begins to cry too and grabs hold of my hand. "I don't know why I do anything anymore." She lets it take her for a moment, then tries to gather herself. We stare at each other, our wet, swollen faces, looking for something.

"Why can't you do like I do? Just stay under the radar?"

"Ellie. You don't even live in your skin." She taps me on the head. "You live in *here.*"

I look to my left at Jimmy Bear, her favorite stuffed animal, with that same surprised expression he's been wearing for at least ten years. We used to laugh and say, "How is it *still* so surprising to him?" We like that he isn't jaded.

"Gwen?" She turns her head to me, ready. "I don't feel real sometimes. Do you know what I mean? Sometimes I just feel like I'm not *real.*"

I see her eyes well up, then she closes them and takes in a deep breath. She squeezes my hand, and in that moment I feel her, and all that is between us. She smiles at me, a sad little smile, then she wipes her face. "Jesus, Ellie," she says. "Not now, okay?"

We hear the police car pull up, and then our mother comes into Gwen's room. She's gotten dressed up for this. She's changed into a black dress and heels. Makeup. *Perfume.*

"Going somewhere?" Gwen asks.

"Yes. After they take you to jail, I'm going out to celebrate."

"You're evil."

"That's right. And don't you ever forget it. Now hurry up." She turns to leave, but then stops and says, "Go wash your face. You look like a mess."

Gwen sighs then stands up to walk out. "I love you," I say.

"God, I'm a fuckup," she says. "You're coming down, right?"

Gwen and I walk downstairs holding hands. It takes me a moment to realize that she hasn't let go. She always lets my hand go when someone else is present, but this time she has forgotten. Or maybe not.

Our mother is sitting in the big, stuffed armchair. She looks like a queen holding court.

"Gwen," she says, "this is Detective Perez."

He stands up from the sofa. "Good evening," he says.

He is a handsome man. Olive skin and thick, dark hair, with a muscular build, dressed simply in a T-shirt and sport coat.

"Girls. Don't just stand there. Sit down." She snaps her fingers at us, motions us toward the loveseat opposite Detective Perez. We sit unusually close. I can hear Gwen's breathing, heavy and trembling.

"Well, let's just start," he says. "Gwen, I am conducting an investigation into the arson at the old mill house. Were you aware that it was burned down last night?"

I feel Gwen's sweaty, shaky hand in mine. She nods her head.

"Was that a yes? I'll need you to answer my questions definitively."

"Yes," she says.

"You know it burned down?"

"Yes. I know it burned down."

"Did you used to go there? Hang out there?"

"Yes."

"Can you tell me what kinds of things you did there?"

Her eyes shift around; she shakes her head, shrugs. "Just stuff," she says.

"Well, I'll need you to be more specific."

"You know . . . we hung out. Listened to music. *Stuff.*"

"Did you consume alcohol?"

"Sometimes."

"What about drugs?"

"I don't do drugs."

"No? What about cigarettes? Do you smoke?"

"Um . . ." She finds our mother with her eyes. "Yes."

Our mother gasps and gives her the dagger eyes. Then she looks at me. "Did you know about this?"

"Me?" I say, startled.

"Ma'am, I'll need to proceed."

She nods her head. "Right. Go ahead."

"Did you ever have any problems with anyone who hung out at the old mill?"

"Problems?"

"Did you have a fight or any altercations with another person who used to hang out there?"

"No," she says adamantly. "Not at all."

"You sure?"

"*Yes.*"

"How are things at school? How are your grades?"

Gwen shrugs again. "I got all Cs this time."

"You got all Cs? Is that good or bad for you?"

"That's good." I hear my mother make that disapproving *tssk* sound and shift in her chair. She gives Gwen a dirty look and shakes her head. Perez ignores it.

"I see. And how are things at home?"

Gwen pauses, breaking the rhythm. She looks at our

mother, then away, plays with the piping on the arm of the loveseat. "I don't know," she says finally.

"You don't know?" he asks, mimicking her slightly.

"They're okay, I guess."

"Is Dad around?"

"Not really."

"Your mom told me you've been having a hard time since he left."

Gwen turns her head quickly to look at our mother. "I guess so," she says.

"Are you on any medication? Anything for depression?"

"I'm not crazy!"

"No, of course not."

"Jesus! What is this? Therapy?"

"Let's just calm down."

"No! What do you want to know? You want to know if I had a grudge against someone? I didn't. I loved it there!" Gwen starts to cry, hides her face in her hands. "I loved it there."

Detective Perez waits for a moment. "Gwen," he says. "Where were you last night, June 16, at approximately ten o'clock?"

Gwen pulls a throw pillow to her chest, clutches it tight. I feel her move away from me, separate now, like she is floating to where no one can reach her. I want to rewind, go back, change all of this. I could rewrite it for her. In my version, she doesn't even go to the old mill. She is home with me, looking through magazines, and it is enough for her.

"Gwen? I'll need an answer. Were you at the old mill house last night?"

Gwen clings to the pillow as tears stream down her face. I start to cry too, and I squeeze her leg with my hand. "It's okay, sissy," I say.

"Detective," our mother says. "As you can see, my daughter is very upset. So let me just save us all some trouble and tell you that Gwen was home last night. All night."

Gwen and I both sit up, like a string has pulled us from above. We look at each other, then at our mother, then back at each other, and with our eyebrows say, *What?*

Perez's jaw tightens. I see his nostrils flare as he turns to look at my mother.

"I am addressing these questions to Gwen, Mrs. Roma."

"It's *Ms.,*" she says, then gives him a smile that I, for one, have never seen. It's amazing how beautiful she is in those moments when the hardness falls away. "Go ahead, Gwen. Tell Detective Perez you were here last night."

Gwen turns to me, her mouth hanging open just a little. I see her face searching for where to go next. She stumbles at first, looks at my mother several times. My mother raises an eyebrow, motions at Gwen with her chin. "Go ahead," she says again. Gwen looks at Perez, swallows hard.

"I was home last night," she manages. "Watching TV."

Our mother's eyes dart over, suggesting she has said too much. Gwen sinks back on the loveseat. Perez leans forward. "Really?" he says. "What did you watch?" I feel my stomach do a swan dive.

My mother leans forward too, looks him right in the eye. "*Dynasty,*" she says, and doesn't look away. She kicks her foot back and forth a bit, allowing her high heel to nearly fall off but then flexing it back up at just the right moment to catch it. She's playing with her shoe. *She's enjoying this.*

Perez takes a deep breath. *"Dynasty?* Gwen, let me guess, is that how you remember it as well?"

Gwen nods her head, then takes the ball and runs. "Yes," she says. "We watched it like we always do. And my mother made popcorn." For a moment I can almost see it, the two of them huddled on the couch watching the saga of the Carringtons, munching on hot, buttered popcorn, frustrated when the story is interrupted by commercial breaks.

"It was just the two of you?"

"Yes. Ellie was at Celia's."

Perez fixes his eyes on me. "You weren't home?"

"No, sir," I say.

He looks at my mother, who is still poised and ready. "So you and Gwen were here alone watching *Dynasty.* Is that right?"

"That's right." Her smile grows a bit more satisfied now.

"What episode was it?"

"Sammi Jo and her scheming, as usual. Blackmail this time."

"Blackmailing who?"

"Crystal. Do you watch the show?"

"No."

"Oh. Well you should watch it sometime. The girls and I try not to miss it." She looks over at us, gives a tight, closed-lip smile, and cocks her head to one side. "Right, ladies?" Gwen and I nod in unison.

"Ms. Roma, I have a witness who says they saw Gwen down at the old mill house last night."

"They're lying."

"Excuse me?"

"I said, they're lying."

"I've been doing this a long time. I think I'd know if a witness were lying."

"Detective Perez, you look much too young to have been doing this a long time. But I know you are very good at what you do, so I guess the witness is simply mistaken."

"The witness placed Gwen at the scene last night."

"And I'm telling you she was home. Now, who are you going to believe? Some drunk teenager, or Gwen's own mother?" My mother adjusts herself in the chair, smoothes her dress with her hands. "Gwen is not a bad kid. She's had some problems this year; she's been having a hard time since her father ran off. But we're working through it. She's making real progress." She looks at Gwen, smiles. "Aren't you, honey?" Then she leans in closer to Perez, her voice thick and seductive. "And besides. Who really cares about an old abandoned building anyway, right?"

Detective Perez closes his notebook and clips his pen in the spiral. He is quiet for a moment, then he looks at my mother. She just stares back. Checkmate.

He gets up from the sofa. "Well. Thank you for your time. I will note our conversation in my report, and if I have any further questions, I'll be in touch."

"Of course," she says. "We'd be happy to help in any way we

can." She stands up to walk him to the door. He looks at Gwen and me, nods. I almost feel sorry for him. "Good night," he says. We all say bye at the same time.

"Thank you for coming by," she calls out to him from the doorway. "Now don't work too hard." She laughs softly, closes the door behind her.

Our mother comes into the living room. "Well," she says, "I think it's time for bed. Why don't you girls go wash your faces." As a reflex, Gwen begins to argue that she'd already washed her face, but she immediately stops herself. Gwen lets go of my hand and follows our mother up the stairs.

I stay behind for a moment, giving them some space, but aware, too, of the shift that has taken place. Alone in the living room, I listen to their footsteps above me, and to my own steady breathing down here below.

eleven

It is June 21, the longest day of the year and also the best one, because it is the last day of school before summer break. I am standing in the hall next to the Science Labs waiting for Celia. She is saying good-bye to Kevin. I am trying not to stare, so I can't give a full report, but from where I stand you'd think it was World War II and Kevin was being shipped off to Normandy. Celia is crying—no, *weeping*. Kevin is holding her face in his hands, saying something soothing.

They have been going steady for exactly five weeks, which, if you think about it, is not a terribly long time. But if you knew Celia, you'd know that five weeks is long enough for them to have named their first child (Toby), selected the name and breed of their dog (Speedbump, a bichon frise), and drawn rough sketches of their dream home. So, if you think of it that way, then you can see that an entire life together is going up in smoke right here in the Science hall.

We walk out of the building together, the three of us. Kevin finally says good-bye and climbs on his bus. Celia's bus hasn't arrived yet.

"You okay?"

She nods. Wipes her face. Stares off for a moment. Then, "Will you write to me?"

"Yes," I say. "I'd love to."

Her bus pulls in. She throws her arms around me. "I'll *miss* you."

"You will?"

"Of course! Why do you sound surprised?"

"Well, I mean, you'll be at *camp*. There's gonna be, like, dances and canoeing and crap."

"I'll still miss you. Will you miss me?"

I look at her face for a moment. The last time I slept at her house we sneaked into the kitchen and got Doritos, pickles, and Keebler Fudge Sticks. We sat outside on the lawn while we ate it, all of it, looked up at the stars and talked about whether Winter White was a pure white or more of an off-white like cream or ivory.

Ours is a delicate dance, mine and Celia's. Several months ago, I came to school with a pretty big cut just above my eyebrow. (Compliments of my mother, who had backhanded me when I asked, rather smartly, I admit, if she had any intention of buying groceries.) I met up with Celia in the bathroom just before first period, saw her survey the cut on my brow bone and look away. Then she quietly handed me her compact for a touch-up. I think, in her way, she was trying to allow me some privacy, trying not to embarrass me or call attention to it. But along with that, I think she spotted something in me, a certain darkness that she just didn't want to get too close to.

"Earth to Ellie!"

"Oh. Sorry."

"So I guess that's a no?"

"What is?"

"To missing me."

"Oh. No. I mean no, it's not a no. I mean *yes*. Jesus!"

She shakes her head and puts her arms around me again. Her blond curls tickle my face. She climbs on the bus, takes her seat, and waves to me out the window. I feel my throat tighten, then bite the tears back.

I stand on the sidewalk as the bus pulls away. Mr. Cole passes me on his way back into the building.

"Well, Ms. Roma." He says it like he has caught me doing something, but I am only waving good-bye.

"Hi, Mr. Cole."

He puts an arm around me; I can smell the coffee on his breath, even though he'd tried to cover it with a Velamint.

"Your sister's a lucky girl," he says.

"Yes, sir."

"Good thing your mother could vouch for her whereabouts."

I nod quickly, looking for the exit sign. "Uh-huh."

He leans in closer. "But probably luckier that the Owens family decided not to press charges, huh?"

I swallow. Feel the blood leave my face. He winks at me.

"You have a good summer now, you hear?"

Across the parking lot, I see Greg. "Yes, sir. I will. Well, I see my ride. I should probably go." I break away from him and head toward the parking lot.

"Stay out of trouble!"

I don't look back until I catch up with Greg. Mr. Cole disappears into the building.

"Hi," I say. "I didn't see you in Study Hall."

It's been tense since the old mill incident. He's been quiet around me, looking at the ground a lot. I'm not mad at him. It isn't his fault he got caught in Hurricane Gwen.

"I had to clean out my locker. Do you need a lift?"

"I do. But . . . do you mind if we don't go home right away?"

"Sure."

He takes the long way home and I look out the window at the big cotton-candy clouds set against a sky so blue it almost hurts to look at it. It doesn't look real to me, more like a painting, more like what a sky is supposed to look like than what it really is. Those giant white masses huddled together, holding on so tightly, then slowly evaporating, letting go at a pace so quiet you don't even notice it.

When we finally pull up to my house and say our good-byes, I feel a tug in him, something he wants to say. He fiddles with a loose thread on the steering wheel.

"Maybe we can . . . hang out sometime. See a movie or something." I look at his face, so benign, and for a moment I wonder what that's like. The movies, and maybe McDonald's. I wonder what we'd talk about, how long we could skate on the surface.

"Yeah. Okay," I say, but I don't really mean it.

"We could see *Can't Buy Me Love.* I heard it's great."

I nod. "That sounds fun." And it does. If I were a different girl. Or from some other place than this one. But I hope he finds someone good to love one day. He really deserves it.

He drives away, and when I go inside I see that our house is full. Gwen has her friends over, so it is wall-to-wall leather jackets, which is something when you consider it's almost a hundred degrees today. For some reason, come summer, our house becomes the place to be with the stoner sect. So much for privacy and introspection.

I avoid the crowd and head upstairs to my mom's room to watch *Laverne and Shirley* reruns on her little TV. They're showing the one where Shirley gets mad at Laverne for wanting to "vo-di-o-do" with a fireman on the first date. Laverne tells her to lighten up and makes herself a glass of milk and Pepsi while Shirley strokes Boo Boo Kitty. Then it occurs to me that I am *so* Shirley.

At around four thirty, I hear the vacuum cleaner running. I go downstairs, and all of them—Gwen, Justina, and Mulletboy—are cleaning! Gwen is Windexing the (wood) coffee table, Justina is doing dishes, and the guy, whose leather jacket has tassels hanging off the arm seams, is vacuuming the carpet. His tassels are whipping around while he covers that carpet like I have never seen. I meet eyes with Gwen, use my hand to close my mouth back up.

"What? Mom's gonna be home, like, any second." She rubs harder at a stain on the table.

We hear the car coming around the corner. It is a good thing we don't have money for her to get that muffler fixed or I swear there would be catastrophic events around here daily. That muffler is the only warning we get.

"Guys! She's coming!"

Within fifteen seconds, cleaning supplies are put away, the air conditioning is turned off, windows are opened back up, pillow cushions are fluffed, and the television is turned off. The mulletboys head for the sliding glass door, then slip out the back. Before he leaves, though, the one with the tassel jacket puts his hand on the back of Gwen's neck and plants the biggest, deepest kiss right on her mouth. It is a soap-opera kiss, but with tongue. He pulls away and she smiles.

"Bye, baby," she says.

"I'll call you later." And he is out the back door.

Our mom opens the front door. Gwen grabs a book and jumps over to the couch. When Mom comes in, Gwen looks up, bored.

"Oh, hey."

"Were you running the air conditioner?"

"Hmm?" Gwen glances up from her book.

"You heard me."

"No." Right back to the book without missing a beat.

My mom looks over at me.

"What're you standing there for?"

"Nothing . . . I was . . ."

"Well, *move*." She walks by me and goes up to her room.

I think of Celia at camp. She's probably at an arts-and-crafts class making candles inside milk cartons or bracelets out of gimp. Or maybe she was horseback riding all day and is resting in her cabin before a group dinner. One thing she did tell me, though, is that there is no hot water for showers, so that's a downside right there. Plus, she said the mosquitoes were killer.

It is about eight o'clock and I am back on the front stoop. We've seen this show before, but I keep coming back for an encore. Maybe I think the show will end differently, but then isn't that what they say about crazy people? Only crazy people do the same thing over and over and expect a different result.

I came outside about an hour ago to walk the block, and when I was finished and tried to go back inside, the door had been locked. Gwen was already gone when I left to go exercise, but my mother was still powdering and perfuming for her date, so I thought I had plenty of time. But somehow I still managed to miss the window of opportunity. The window's locked too. I guess the sane thing would be to start expecting this to happen, to live as though every time I walked out my front door I would end up locked out. But it doesn't happen every time, just sometimes. In Biology, Mrs. Price told us about an experiment they did with chickens. One group of chickens was fed every time they pecked, another group was fed every second time, and the third group was fed at random. When the food was cut off, the first group stopped trying immediately, and the second group stopped soon afterward. The third group, on the other hand, *never stopped trying*. It's the unpredictability of things; that's what gets you.

I had walked around the block six times doing what is called a Power Walk, where you pump your arms real hard as you go. It kind of makes you look like a pissed-off old lady in a big hurry. I had seen the other neighborhood ladies do it, so I gave it a try. I'm hoping it will make my arms more toned. One thing we do as women is focus on the parts that need the most improvement; in my case this would be my lower body, but we have to remember that the whole package is important.

The sun is finally gone and the street lamps have just come on. It got up to ninety-seven degrees today, but with the humidity it felt more like a thousand. The air has cooled off a bit, but that thick wetness is still hanging on like it's got something to prove, and the honeysuckle and fresh cut grass are fighting each other for center stage.

I am watching ants trek across a crack in the sidewalk when I look up and see Leo emerging from his house. It is funny what happens inside you. Normally, I am happy, yet this time my first thought is that I want to run inside before he sees me. It is nothing against Leo; it is purely a vanity thing. The humidity makes my hair take the form of a small shrub, and with the six blocks I just hoofed, I no doubt look like a glazed doughnut to boot. I turn to go, but then I remember the door. Maybe he won't come over.

Well, here he comes. By the way, I'm wearing white overall shorts that are too small, meaning they are tight and constantly riding up instead of slouchy and casual like overalls should be. Oh, and I'm also wearing *Keds*. Old, tired Keds that have been washed in the machine too many times, so the toe part is warped. My feet look like they are yawning.

"Hey," he says as he gets closer. He unwraps a pack of Marlboro Reds and taps them on the back of his hand. His hair is pulled back in a low ponytail, with the shorter pieces falling in little wisps around his face.

"Hi, Leo." My smile feels apologetic, like I am sorry that I don't look my best.

He smiles, nods his head. He lights his cigarette, takes a drag, and blows the smoke over his shoulder to avoid blowing it on me.

"You finished with school?"

"Yes. Today."

"No more math for a while."

"Nope. Thank *God.*"

He stares off for half a second. I notice there is stubble on the very bottom part of his chin. He props his foot up on the step below me, rests his hand on his thigh. There is a tension on his face I haven't seen before.

"What do you think about this place, Ellie?"

"What place? You mean Maryland?"

"Yes."

"Well. I'm not sure. I feel mixed about it, really."

"I think it sucks, personally."

"I don't know. Parts of it are beautiful. Y'know? It's so green all the time, and there's always something about to bloom, or a season about to change. It's like it's always making a promise to you. I like that about it. And the people, well, they seem *friendly* enough. But there seems to be a box that they live in and think in and even dress in, and I don't think I fit inside it."

He measures my words for a moment. Nods his head just slightly in what appears to be agreement.

"I mean, I'm not an expert or anything. I don't even have anything to compare it to. But it just seems to me that there's got to be a place out there where who you've been and where you come from aren't as important as who you become. A person's got to be able to reinvent themselves once in a while, don't you think?"

He nods his head and I see a smile appear at the corner of his mouth. I cross my legs, Indian-style, tuck my Keds beneath me.

"Well, I should get going," he says. "You staying out here?"

"Yes."

"How come?"

His question catches me off guard and I stammer a little. "I . . . uh . . . it's . . . really hot in there."

"In your house?"

"Yes."

"Don't you have air conditioning?"

"Oh. We're not allowed to use it. . . ."

"It was almost a hundred degrees today."

"Oh, it's okay. I like it out here. The fireflies will be out soon. . . ."

"Go turn it on now, and then it will be cool when you're ready to go inside." He takes a step toward my front door.

"It's okay, really. . . ." But before I can finish, he has tried the knob.

"The door's locked." I nod my head yes. "Did your mom go out?"

"She'll be right back."

Leo searches my face for a minute, looking for clues. I have just discovered something worse than being ignored. He smiles in an effort to undo it all. He backs up a little. "Okay, then," he says.

I try to lighten it too. I wave him off and say, "Good-*bye,*" like he is a nagging grandma.

Leo gets in his van and backs out of the parking space. He waves to me out the window and I hear the music trail off and watch his red lights fade as he disappears over the hill. Just then, the first firefly blinks its light, then another. Within a minute the darkness is filled with fireflies, twinkling their silent melody. I think about all the people in the world, how each of us has a place where we belong. I wonder then what my place looks like. Because I am not there, and I am not sure I have ever seen it.

Just then Leo's van turns the corner and starts heading toward me. He is coming back. He slows down and pulls up alongside the curb. Then he rolls down his window.

"Why don't you come with me?"

I shake my head and look away; I can't quite form words. I am embarrassed and excited all at once. But instinctively, my mouth begins to say no. Leo stops me.

"Ellie," he says. "I *want* you to."

Even the little hairs on my legs do a double take. I look up at the street lamp to make sure it's getting this.

"Well, I . . ."

He reaches over and opens the passenger side door for me. "Come on. Jump in."

I climb into the van, pull my seat belt around me. "Where are we going?"

"To band practice."

He hits the accelerator and off we go, disappearing over the same hill I'd just watched him go over. In the tape deck, he is playing Van Halen's "Fair Warning."

"You like Van Halen?" he says above the music and David Lee Roth's improvisational grunting.

"Sure," I say. As in *Right now I like everything.* He turns it up just a little and plays along with the drummer on the steering wheel.

Leo speeds up to run a yellow light, then winks at me. He turns up the radio and we fly away down the hill, across the main road, and into the rest of the night. The windows are down and the air is warm and thick whipping past us. Tiny raindrops appear on the windshield, and then I feel them on my arm. They are only dewy little drops and they feel good on my skin. Leo winds up his window just a little, but I leave mine down, lean my elbow out a bit. I can smell the pavement now as we ride across it. It's been baking in the sun all day. Now the rain comes to relieve it and the smell rises up to meet us, filling the whole car. I settle back in my seat, take a deep breath. Get it in there good.

• • •

After about twenty minutes, I think we are somewhere in Potomac, the rich part of the county. We pull into a long, lighted driveway and follow it up to one of the largest homes I have ever seen. It is a huge, white colonial-style house with four enormous white columns. The front door is bright red. There is a gate at the entrance of the driveway and the house is all lit up with tiny spotlights. There are even lights on the yard so that you can see the landscaping. There are Japanese maple trees and tiny manicured evergreens placed in groupings like little islands. When we get out of the van, I notice a split-rail fence to the left, with horses grazing just beyond it. Just then a little dog, a Jack Russell terrier, comes out to greet us. The hair is up on its back.

"Hey, Kip." The dog smoothes his coat down and starts wagging his tail, then comes over and sniffs Leo's pants. Leo leans down and pets his head. Kip comes over to check me out. He stands up on his hind legs and starts pawing at me to pick him up. I reach down and haul him up; he immediately starts licking my face, which makes me laugh, so he plants a few licks on my teeth.

"You must be a dog person. Only dog people let dogs lick their face."

"Oh, I love it! Puppy breath is like the best smell on earth. They should bottle it. Sell it."

Leo smiles, nods his head slightly. "Eau de Puppy Breath. I like it. I'm not much for cats, though."

"No, me neither. Cats always seem to me like they're just tolerating you. You know what I mean? They always kind of look at you with this face that says, 'If I were bigger, I'd eat you.'"

He stops walking for a second. "You're funny," he says. And I feel his eyes linger on me for a moment. Then he starts walking again.

"Leo? Where *are* we?"

Slowing down so I can catch up with him, he says, "Drummer's house. His *parents'* house, actually."

I follow Leo toward the garage, around the side of the house, and down some dark stairs. We walk into what I guess is the basement, except it is all finished on one side like a little apartment. There is a small kitchen area and a screen between the couch and the bed. Just beyond the apartment area is a cement floor, the walls here are unfinished, with exposed piping and that pink fiberglass stuff. Over on that side I can see music equipment. A set of drums on a riser, a few microphones, and five Marshall amplifiers.

There are three other guys and two girls sitting on the sofa when we walk in. I recognize one of them as the pink-bikini girl from the pool.

"Superstar!" One of the guys holds his arm up; he's holding a bottle of Heinekin. "Glad you could make it."

Leo ignores him, sets his guitar down. The two girls do a simultaneous *Hi*. They both have long, blond hair: One's is stick-straight with bangs, the other's is permed and teased, and all of it is pushed over to one side. The straight-haired girl is wearing a bright orange tank top and a black miniskirt with black cowboy boots. The permed girl has on a black leotard top that comes slightly off her shoulders and a pair of shredded-up, acid-washed jeans.

The guy with the beer stands up. He is wearing a white tank top and tight purple pants. His hair is beautiful. Long, wavy, and jet-black. Kind of like Gwen's.

"Who's your friend?" Up until now I'd been kind of hoping I could just blend in with the furniture, go completely unnoticed. Or maybe go outside and hang with Kip.

"This is Ellie." Everyone says hello. I wave back. I hear the girls say *aww,* like I am a kid who has stumbled into the room wearing those pajamas with the feet.

Leo introduces everyone to me by name. The one with bangs is Tina; the one with the perm, the pool chick, is Bonnie. The guy with the beer is Bones. The other two guys are Flipper and Eddie. They are the rest of the band.

Flipper has a shock of bleached hair. It is about six inches long and sticks out evenly all over his head, the finger-in-the-light-socket look. "So, can we start or what?"

Everyone takes their places. Leo stands in front! He is the singer as well as one of the guitar players. Kip comes in through the dog door. He comes over, looks up at me expectantly, and wags his tail. I pat my lap and he jumps up. When no one is looking, I sniff his little paw for that familiar corn-chip smell.

Bonnie stands up and goes to get a beer out of the fridge. Tina leans in to me.

"I'm Eddie's girlfriend," she says. "The *drummer.*"

"Oh." I nod my head enthusiastically. "He seems nice."

"Have you ever seen the guys play?" I shake my head no.

"Really? Well, you're gonna love 'em. They're gonna be really big stars. Everyone says Eddie is the next Rikki Rockett."

Bonnie comes back over and sits down. Tina tells her this is my first time seeing the band.

"That's so . . . *cute*," she says.

"What are they called?"

They both look at me as though I've asked if they know who the president is. Bonnie is a little beside herself. She fluffs her crunchy curls.

"They're called Vandal."

"Vandal? Oh, *Vandal*. Right." I've never heard of them.

Bonnie takes a swig of beer and scans my entire body with just her eyes. "How do you know Leo?"

"He's my neighbor."

She throws a look at Tina. It is one of satisfaction and relief. Though she may have suspected it before, it is clear to her now that she can go ahead and count me out of the competition.

Bones starts to play some notes on his guitar, nonsensical, really. I think he is tuning it up. Leo is doing a minipace, just three steps in each direction, waiting for Bones to finish.

"Let's do 'House of Love' first," Leo says. Tina and Bonnie clasp hands excitedly. Tina pats my knee. "You'll *love* this." The drummer, Eddie, counts down by tapping his sticks together.

The song is slow, a ballad. Bonnie and Tina sway back and forth. Even with all that is going on, I am unable to look at anyone but Leo. There is a sudden calm to him. His eyes are closed and he is right up at the microphone; his lips touch it now and again. He is strumming out chords on his guitar, but other than that, he is perfectly still. It is as though he has to be still so that he can contain all that is going on inside of him and guide it out smoothly through his voice and his hands. Occasionally, a mixture of pain and pleasure will show up on his face, revealing all that is going on underneath.

I have such a strange feeling in me. It is a kind of . . . duplicitous ache, like I am being pulled toward Leo and held back from him all at once. Seeing him up there, I am so aware of his tremendous capacity for feeling. I want to run to him, search all of his corners, and see if maybe there is room for me in any of them. But at the same time, I am held back by the fear that there would certainly not be. And yet, it is that same . . . *remoteness* that pulls me back toward him and won't let go.

At certain moments during the song he opens his eyes, and because I am sitting right there, he looks at me. Elvis did this very same thing. Priscilla had gone to his house in Germany to meet him, and although there were dozens of people there, Elvis had turned his body away from the piano and sung "Are You Lonesome Tonight?" right to her. She had smiled at him self-consciously, perfecting a mixture of shyness and openness, so I do too, because looking away from Leo is not a possibility.

When the song ends, Leo bows his head a little, then looks up and smiles. Tina and Bonnie erupt into applause. Bonnie leans over and says, "He is *too* hot."

Leo leaves the microphone and walks over to me, his guitar still strapped to him. He pets Kip's head.

"You were great," I say.

"Did you like it?" I nod my head yes.

"Hey, lover boy!" Bones yells across the room. "Ya wanna come back here and play another one?"

Bonnie smiles at me with closed lips; she blinks slowly.

Well. I may be the clueless neighbor in Keds, but as of right now, I am back in the race. It is every woman for herself.

It is nearly eleven o'clock by the time we leave. We drive past the houses with the sweeping front lawns, lit up so well that even at night you can see the diagonal marks left by the lawnmowers. We wind our way through the county until we are nearly home.

I can tell when we are getting close because the houses are lower and the lawns smaller. This increases exponentially until you get to my neighborhood, where all the homes are attached to one another. There, up on the hill, I see it. The rows of brick-and-wood boxes, the tiny patches of grass. The lone street lamp. Her car out front.

I feel that familiar sensation rush over me, like it is time to hide now. This always happens before I go back there. I suddenly feel whoever I have been out here in this world doing a contortionist trick to fit back into what I am supposed to be there, in that world.

Leo pulls into his parking space and turns off the engine.

"Home again," I say.

"Yes," he says sarcastically. "Our favorite place."

We say good-bye and I go around back to crawl in through the window and see Gwen sitting on the couch watching TV. I tap lightly on the glass and she jumps. She comes and opens the sliding glass door for me.

"You scared the shit out of me."

"Sorry." I close the door quietly behind me. She sits back down, then motions at my Big Gulp with her chin. "Where'd you get that?"

"7-Eleven."

"I know *that*." She changes the channel with the remote. "Who did you go with?"

I search her face for the go-ahead. Carefully, I say, "Leo."

"Who's that? Wait . . . the guy from the pool?"

I nod in affirmation.

"He took you out?"

"I was locked out."

"Right. Charity case. Fun, huh? Nice mom we have. Locking her kids out of their own damn house." She holds out her hand for me to give her my drink. She takes a sip from the straw. "Eewww." She wrinkles up her nose. "You got *diet*?" Then she takes another sip.

I look at the TV. She's watching *Headbanger's Ball* on MTV.

"Well," she says as though it is an afterthought. "You missed some big excitement around here tonight."

"Oh?"

"Yeah. Mom had some dude in her room."

"You mean Reggie?"

"No. Someone *else*."

"Is he still here?"

"No, he left a little while ago. Nice, huh?"

Jon Bon Jovi comes on the TV. His long, shaggy hair is wrapped in a colorful scarf, and he is dancing around with his mike stand, pyrotechnics exploding in the background. This guy, I'm thinking, can't hold a candle to Leo.

We hear her door open, her footsteps coming down the stairs. Gwen turns the TV down, a preventive measure. She comes into the living room anyway. She is wearing her royal blue night-gown with the cap sleeves. She squints at me, adjusting her eyes to the light.

"Have you been here all night?"

"Me?" I point to myself. "Yes. Uh-huh." She just nods and turns to walk away when Gwen says, "Hey, Mom?" She turns back to us.

"What?"

"I was just wondering," she says, "why the back of your hair is all matted."

Gwen! It is too much, how she is. It is too much! I cringe with the force of lightning.

Our mother cranes her neck up so she can look down at us even more.

"Don't worry about it, you little smartass."

"Oh, okay. 'Cause I was just wondering, y'know, like *why* your hair would be all matted. I thought you'd like to explain that to your *daughters.*"

She stares at Gwen in silence for a moment, then slowly walks over to her and leans down. She points her finger in Gwen's face, close enough so that just the tip of her acrylic nail touches the end of Gwen's nose.

"Let me tell *you* something, you little bitch. I got something on you. Remember? How about I call the police, tell them where you really were. Huh? How about that?"

Gwen's eyes start to tear. My mother leans back in satisfaction. "That's what I thought."

Well. There it is. What had seemed like an instinctive, shielding rescue had in fact been a capture.

We hear her go into the kitchen, pour herself some iced tea, and go back upstairs. When we hear the door close, Gwen allows the tears to fall.

"Why is she *so mean* to me?" She cries into her hands. "What did I do to her? I don't under*stand.*"

I put my hand on her back and sip my Big Gulp. She's not really asking me, anyway. She's just allowing a rare moment of despair. Besides, there isn't any reason as to why our mother is the way she is to us. I imagine it is not even about us, really; she would be this way to anyone who would let her. This latest episode, this threat she has to hold over Gwen's head, is just her way of digging her talons in deeper and keeping Gwen close. And there isn't any reason in particular why she chose Gwen to latch onto; it's that Gwen simply exposed her soft underbelly first, creating the opportunity for my mother to seize her.

By the time I go to my room, it is nearly two A.M. The moon outside is bright enough for me to make it to my bed without turning on the light. Outside, the crickets are madly rubbing their tiny legs together in hopes that another cricket might take notice of them.

I survey the contents of my room in the moonlight: my twin

bed pushed along the far wall, the red plastic milk crate turned upside down as my nightstand. Across from my bed on a small wooden table is my record player. It's part of the stereo system my parents had in the basement back in Boonesville. Gwen got the radio and tape deck and I got the turntable. I love the turntable best, anyway. I used to lie on the floor in our basement and listen to my REO Speedwagon records. I got the *High Infidelity* album for Christmas, and I would go down there every day, press my head down on the lime green shag carpet, and listen to the music. I loved the warm, fuzzy sound of the needle on the record so much I wished I could crawl inside it. But mostly it was the lyrics that got me. The songs were about love letters, betrayals, and efforts to reaffirm the love that had gone awry. I would lie there on the basement floor for hours, allowing the bass to throb through my body, and I'd wonder when on earth this was going to happen for me. When would I have love of my own? I just *couldn't wait* for my life to happen. And now, it appears that it has begun.

I lie down on my bed and watch the walnut tree's shadow on the wall. Then I think about earlier, driving with Leo, and start to play it over in my head. The way I always do.

After something happens, I find a quiet place and start to sort through all that is new in my mind. As though I were an archeologist, I gently excavate each event, carefully dusting off every word and every glance. After I've extracted each moment, I take them one by one and hold them to the light, examining each one like it was a rare skeletal fragment of a velociraptor, only much more valuable. At least to me.

Here's one I study for a while: At the 7-Eleven, Leo was paying for our Big Gulps when he nudged me with his elbow and motioned to the guy over at the magazine rack. I looked over at the man, who was wearing a neon green tank top and running shorts. His hair was perfectly coifed, all of the layers turning neatly upward so that he looked like a frosted Q-tip.

"Who's he look like?" Leo said under his breath.

"That's easy," I said. "Barry Manilow."

"I dare you to go over there and start singing 'Mandy.'"

"No way! You do it."

"Are you daring me?" He raised his left eyebrow slightly and started walking over to the magazines, humming softly, *"Oh Mandy. Well you came and you gave without taking. . . ."*

"No! Stop. Don't! Oh, my God!" And I began laughing uncontrollably, my Big Gulp trembling in my hand.

We left the 7-Eleven and got back into the van. Before starting the engine, Leo turned to me and said, "It's your turn. Truth or dare?"

"When did we start playing Truth or Dare?"

"Inside. You dared me, and I did it, so now it's your turn."

"No, *you* dared *me* and I *didn't* do it. . . ."

"Quit stalling."

"Oh, *God*. Okay. *Truth*."

He took a sip of his drink and stared ahead for a moment. Then he turned to me and said, "Okay. Tell the truth . . . Did you or did you not know that when you smile, I mean when you *really* smile, you have a very cute little dimple on your left cheek?"

• • •

I get up from my bed and open my window. I take a sip of my Big Gulp and set it back down, returning it to the sweaty ring it has made on the milk crate. I lie back down and watch Leo's face in my mind, watch his mouth move to form the words. He'd paused after he said it, as if he were making sure I'd received it. I did receive it, felt it travel into the smallest parts of me, and then I felt my breath leave me, and I felt all the blades of grass stand on end to pay attention. And in that moment, I felt the whole wide world open up, felt it get bigger.

I reach my hand up to my face, run my fingertips over my left cheek. I make a smile and feel around for the tiny groove. Then I feel the whole big world come into my room and say, *You see? You are not alone after all.*

twelve

"Gwen, hurry the fuck up. You look fine." Justina is sitting on Gwen's bedroom floor, burning off the stray fringes from the hem of her jeans with a green Bic lighter. Gwen is trying on outfits. They are getting ready to go to a concert.

"This is not a good idea," I say. "You're still grounded."

"Do I give a shit? *She* is not going to stop me from seeing Kix play Hammerjack's. No way."

Gwen puts on a pair of denim short-shorts and a black lace bustier. "What about this one?"

"That's hot," Justina says. "Do you have any gloves? That'd be killer."

Gwen opens her drawers and starts rummaging around.

"Ellie, have you seen my gloves?"

"Which ones?"

"The long, black ones."

"The ones you wore to the Christmas Formal? You're wearing *those*?"

"It's a hot look," Justina assures me.

I shouldn't press my luck, because it's amazing that I'm even in here. Since the whole old mill thing, Gwen and Justina let me hang around more. They think I acted cool about it, and it scored me some much-needed points.

"Here they are." Gwen pulls the silky gloves from her bottom drawer and begins to pull them over her dark, skinny arms. She strikes a pose.

"Very Lita," Justina says.

"Who?" I ask.

"Lita Ford. She's a guitar player." Justina lights a cigarette. "I'm gonna learn guitar, man. Gwen, you gotta talk your mom into buying you a bass. We'll start an all-girl group."

"Like the Runaways."

"Exactly."

"That'd be cool as shit. Should I wear my cowboy boots or my white spiked booties?"

"That's a tough one."

"Ellie?"

"Um . . ." I am completely unprepared to be asked for my opinion. The question feels enormous. One wrong move and I am banished to the no-man's-land of my own adjacent bedroom. "I vote for the cowboy boots. White shoes will clash with the rest of your outfit."

"Maybe I should wear a white bustier instead? And the

booties with white lace socks! Oh, that's good." Gwen begins
to get undressed.

"Dude, you gotta hurry up." Justina puts her cigarette out in
her soda can. "It's already seven o'clock and we still have to
pick up Michelle."

"Yeah, just one more second."

"Who are you guys going to see again?"

"Kix. Your little friend is going. Will you tie me?" I go over and
lace up the back of the white bustier. "What little friend?" Gwen
puts on white bobby socks with lace trim like we used to wear
when we were kids, and her white, pointy ankle boots with the
spiked heels. "Foxy Boy from the pool. What's his name again?
Leo." I feel my hands start to tremble at the sound of his name.

"How do you know?"

"I saw him outside earlier." She turns a few times. "This is
too Madonna, isn't it?" she asks.

"Dude, you're fine. But lose the gloves now."

"No gloves?"

"Not unless you have white ones. Just hurry or we won't get
in. We still have to pick up Michelle."

"You got the IDs didn't you?"

"Yeah. But still. I don't want any problems. I'm going to call
Michelle and tell her to be ready."

Justina goes to use the phone in our mother's room. She
just left for her date twenty minutes ago. Justina had hidden
around the corner until our mom left. Gwen's not allowed to
hang out with her anymore. It's part of her punishment for
the old mill.

Justina walks back into the room with a puss on. "Michelle can't go."

Gwen turns away from the mirror. "What?"

"Her fucking mom found her bong."

"Shit. That ticket cost thirty bucks."

"I know. Fucking drag. We're gonna have to scalp her ticket and sell her fake ID." Justina pulls the IDs from her pocket and throws them on the vanity. One of the girls, Sheila is her name, kind of looks like me. Well, if I were older and had a different haircut, that is. But if I worked at it a little, I could be her. And then Leo could see me and he would say, *Now who is that?* And then I would turn around in slow motion, the wind blowing on me just right, and in a throaty voice I'd say, *Why it's me, Leo. It's* me.

"Hey, you guys?" I hear myself say. "Do you think I could pass for her?"

Gwen is applying Tatiana perfume and stops mid-spritz. "What?"

Justina puts down Gwen's Rubik's Cube even though she almost got two colors. "What?"

"You guys, I have to go. I'm in love. Please, Gwen. I'm dying inside!"

Justina looks at Gwen. "Dude, what is wrong with her?"

"Please, Gwen. Please. Make me look older. Make me look hot. Please."

Gwen goes back to applying black eyeliner. She looks at me in the mirror. "No way, Ellie. You'll get us busted." She begins teasing her hair. I feel my desperation mounting.

"I will tell Mom!" I say, but they just look at me like I'm a gnat. I point my finger so they know I mean business. "I will tell Mom on you! I will!" Gwen stops teasing her hair.

"You are such a pain in my ass," she says, and as I hold the look on my face I see her fold. *"Fine."*

Justina throws herself on the bed. "Oh, Jesus," she says.

Gwen points her comb at me. "But I swear to God, Ellie, if you act like a dork—"

"I won't! I swear to God! I will not be dorky! Just . . . fix me, okay? Make me hot. Like a . . . like a rocker babe."

Gwen rolls her eyes and motions for me to come over. She gets a sinister but very pleased-looking grin on her face and takes me by the shoulders. "We're going to corrupt you," she says with a laugh. "Let me dress you."

Justina crosses her arms. "I don't believe this."

"It's gonna be great." Gwen cheers. "We're corrupting Ellie!"

"You have five minutes," Justina concedes. Then she shakes her head and smiles. "Hurry. If I miss the show I am never speaking to either of you again."

Gwen goes into her closet and throws out various things for me try on, but the only one that fits is a black minidress, which is even a little flattering because it's like wearing a girdle.

"You've lost weight, Ellie. Seriously. You look great."

"I didn't know you had such big tits," Justina offers.

"I feel like a sausage. Is this leather?" I try to pull the hemline down and the top part up.

"Not exactly."

Gwen returns to her closet to look for shoes. We wear almost the exact same shoe size, which is something I will require of all my future roommates. She holds up a black pump and a turquoise scrunch boot with a studded ankle belt.

"Which ones?"

"The boots," Justina says. "She's not used to heels. You have three minutes, and then I'm leaving both of you."

Gwen ushers me over to the bed and starts applying makeup to my face. She keeps looking at the picture ID of Sheila as a reference, then comes at me with more. Over and over she traces my eyes and rubs shadow on my lids. Then she teases my hair, pulling the sides away from my head and affixing them with copious amounts of Sebastian Spritz Forte. She leans in close to me to line my lips, and I breathe in a nearly fatal dose of her Tatiana perfume. I glance up and my eyes meet hers. She smiles at me, pleased.

"Why are you being so nice to me?" I ask.

"Because you're letting me."

"Breakfast Club!" Justina yells, and she and Gwen both start laughing.

I stand up to look at myself in the mirror.

"Wow."

"What do you think?"

"Wow," I say again.

"The train is leaving. All aboard!"

"Okay, okay."

Justina leaves and Gwen begins to follow her out. I pause for a moment. "What's wrong?" she asks.

"I'm scared."

She smiles and reaches her hand out to me. "Come on, pretty girl," she says. " I won't let anything happen to you."

It is all I have ever wanted, this moment. That sentence. She takes me by the hand and leads me out the door. What will happen from here on I don't know. And for once, I don't really care.

We pile into Justina's car. We look like the girls from that ZZ Top video. Just wait until Leo sees this. He will wonder, *Bonnie who?*

We get in the car, me in back of course, and drive out of the neighborhood. Gwen lights a cigarette with the car lighter, then offers me the pack. I take a cigarette from the pack and allow her to light it for me. I take a tiny drag and erupt in a coughing fit. "Went down the wrong pipe," I say, and they laugh. I am careful not to inhale again.

The air outside is the usual thick and sticky summertime air, all the more noticeable now with full-face makeup and a pleather tube dress. But it doesn't bother me. I love this feeling, when it's eight o'clock and the sun is still up. The tank is full and the wind whips past us as we cruise along the highway, the whole evening before us like a question waiting to be answered.

Justina turns on the radio; they are playing "Wait" by White Lion. Gwen turns it up. "I love this song!" I love this song too, but I've never said so because I thought she would make fun of me. She usually likes the darker stuff. Then there we are, the three of us, singing in unison, *"Wait! Wait! I never had a chance to love you. . . ."*

Gwen turns around to me. "How do you know this song?" she asks.

"You're not the only one who watches MTV," I say. She smiles and our voices fill the car again, terribly off-key and absolutely perfect. Then there is also the sound, audible only to me, of the little songbird in my chest, just tweeting away.

We pull into the gravel parking lot at Hammerjack's. It is already full with Camaros and Z28s, music blasting from within as people knock back cans of beer. I scan the lot for white vans. We wobble on the gravel and take our place at the back of the line. Justina sees her friend Pete is working the door. She looks at me, all business.

"You have your ID memorized?"

"Yes. I'm Sheila Dumphries, I live in Spotsylvania County, I'm twenty-nine years old and I'm a Scorpio."

"You're a Scorpio? What's that got to do with anything?"

"No, *I'm* not a Scorpio, Sheila is. In case they ask. What sign is your girl?"

Justina turns to Gwen. "Dude. Your sister is such a goober."

We get to the front of the line, and Pete, a gorilla of a man with a cropped, military haircut, says hello to Justina. He gives Gwen the once-over, and his face lights up in approval. We show him our IDs one by one. He glances down at Sheila, then up at me. My heart is pounding.

"Have fun, ladies," he says finally, and unlatches the velvet rope. Once we are inside, we do high-fives all around. I don't hesitate when it is my turn to high-five; I do it like it's regular to me.

"Let's try to get closer to the stage," Justina says. We make a chain with our hands, and Gwen and I follow her through the crowd. We get about five feet from the stage before the crowd becomes impassible.

What's hard about this is how much is going on all around me. My brain is being pulled in several different directions, so it's hard to choose what to focus on. The air is thick with cigarette smoke and bodies are pressed up together, creating minisaunas. I stand on my tippy-toes and take inventory of the room. Leo would be one of the tallest people here, for sure, but I don't find his head rising up from the rest of the crowd. The smoke stings my eyes and the floor vibrates beneath me. I look around again. No Leo. Suddenly the house lights go to black, and several white lights pulse from above the stage. The crowd starts to cheer.

"I can't see," Justina says. Then a voice comes booming from the speakers: *Ladies and gentleman. Please welcome Baltimore's own, the kings of noise . . . Please put your hands together for Kix!!* The crowd erupts and the stage explodes into lights and sound and smoke. When the smoke begins to settle, I see five men onstage jumping around, spinning their long hair in a choreographed frenzy. The drummer is standing and thrashing his head around like a windmill, the guitar players are twirling their guitars around their bodies by the straps. For a moment I forget myself, forget Gwen and Justina, and just before panic can set in, I look to my left and see Gwen singing along to every word: *"Red lite! Green lite! TNT . . ."* I look to my right and see feet dangling from a guy's shoulders. I look up, and it is Justina, high above the crowd, hands in the air. She reaches her hands down and then she lifts her shirt up, flashing her breasts to the stage. The crowd cheers her on and the singer acknowledges with a thumbs-up.

As the band plays, each song seems to get louder. I tear off a piece of cocktail napkin and wad it into two little balls for my ears. I don't know the music, but I kind of like it. I like the way it demands that you react, the way it insists you be swept away by it.

I picture Leo up there, how he would do it. Not so flashy, probably, but with the same intensity, the same swagger. One day, when it is his turn, I will stand up there with him—off to the side of the stage, of course. There is a group of girls up there now. That will be me. And I won't pull any of that clingy-girlfriend stuff. I'll be very supportive and I will come to every show, even if I have a cold.

"Thank you! Good night!" The band walks off the stage and the house lights come back up. Justina climbs down from the guy's shoulders and we file out the side doors with the rest of the crowd and spill out into the parking lot.

"That rocked!" Justina says. But her voice sounds like it's underwater. I remove the cocktail napkins from my ears.

I scan the crowd again for Leo. "I don't think he's here," Gwen says. "I looked for him too." This dress is more like a tourniquet than an actual garment, and I've been wearing it for close to four hours. And now to think it was for nothing, well, that's just rude.

"Wait," she says. "Isn't that . . ."

I look over and there he is, standing with Bonnie in a small group. She is wearing a leopard minidress. No Keds for me this time. It is curtains for you.

I smooth my dress and turn to Gwen. "How do I look?" And with that I feel my inner femme fatale emerge. I put one leg in front of the other and walk toward him. "Ellie, don't—" I hear her say, but I keep going. I fluff my bangs.

When I walk up, Bonnie gives me the once-over. Instead of shrinking, I stand straighter.

"Hi, Leo," I say. I see his eyes scan me before he says hello.

"Nice outfit," Bonnie says, and she laughs; some of the others laugh too. But not Leo.

"Ellie, what are you doing?" he says. "Why are you dressed like that? You're just a kid." The sledgehammer to my insides. Digestive paralysis.

Gwen appears beside me. Bonnie laughs again. "Yeah," she scoffs. "Isn't it past your bedtime?" The group laughs with her. There is a girl pointing at my shoes. I look down, but there is nothing. Only that this is wrong. I am all wrong.

Gwen takes a step toward Bonnie. She gets in her face. "You got a problem, bitch?" Bonnie rolls her eyes and steps back a little. "I don't have time for this," she says, bored. Then she reaches out for Leo's hand. He pauses, but then he takes it and I feel my insides break into tiny pieces. He looks at me, his face so sorry. "You're a good girl, Ellie," he says. "You shouldn't be here. Go home." Gwen reaches for me, but I pull away. I don't know why I do that. "Fuck them," she says.

She scans the parking lot. "Where's Justina?"

From across the parking lot I hear, "Gwen!" We both look over and see Justina, standing on the stairs of the tour bus that is parked behind the club. "Come on!"

Gwen starts laughing. "That girl is fucking crazy!" she says. She looks at me, "Come on, sister. We've got *real* musicians to hang out with." She pulls me with her and we run toward the bus. I look over my shoulder, watching Leo and Bonnie walk away.

We climb on the tour bus, and right in front of us, sitting at a little dinette table, is a naked man with long, bleached-blond hair eating a bowl of Fruit Loops, a small pillow in his lap. I look away, pretending not to notice his nakedness, though he seems perfectly comfortable. So does everyone else.

There are a few people sitting on the couches smoking and drinking bottles of Heineken. Toward the end of the couch Justina lies tangled in the arms of the lead singer. She stands up.

"There they are!" she says, and the singer smacks her on the butt. She laughs and pushes him playfully. He grabs her and turns her over his knee. I can hear her squeal. He picks her up and puts her over his shoulder and carries her to the back of the bus. "Save me!" she yells, her face red from laughing.

Next thing I know, Gwen is moving after her. One of the guys from the couch area grabs her from behind, wraps his arms around her waist, and guides her to the back of the bus. The rest of the group follows, and I am left at the front with Naked Man as Gwen and Justina disappear behind the door.

"Have a seat," he says, his mouth full of Fruit Loops. I take the seat farthest away and try to look at anything but him. My cuticles are suddenly fascinating.

The bathroom door opens and a man comes out, still zipping up his red leather pants. I recognize him as the drummer. He also has blond hair, but I think his is the color he was born with, more golden than white or yellow. He has a nice, chiseled face and a mole right where Marilyn Monroe did. His eyes are light green, leaning more toward blue than gold like mine and Gwen's do. He has no shirt on, just a white towel around his neck. I guess people don't like clothes around here. Must be hard to do laundry or something.

He heads toward the front of the bus, then sees me and stops. I think I am in his way, so I scoot my feet in so he can pass. He smiles and points at me.

"Do I know you?"

I point to myself. "Me?"

"Yeah. *You.* Stage left about four rows back, right?"

"That's right," I say, and feel my face redden.

"What's your name?"

"Ellie." I say quickly, remembering my promise not to be dorky.

He holds out his hand. "Hi, Ellie. I'm Ratchett." Big, white teeth.

Through his Fruit Loops, Naked Man chimes in, "His real name's Aaron."

Ratchett looks at me guiltily and shrugs. "It's true."

"That's Elvis's middle name," I say.

"Why, yes, it is." He flicks his towel at Naked Man. "See? The lady knows a good name when she hears it." He turns to me. "Ignore him." Then he asks, "Do you like Elvis?"

"Yes."

"Do you think he's still alive?"

"Oh. I don't know."

"Well, that's what they're sayin'. It's all over the TV. A woman in Georgia claims she saw him at the Piggly Wiggly."

"Really?"

He sits down next to me on the couch. "Yep. She says she's sure it was him, except his hair was blond. Elvis had blond hair naturally. Did you know that?"

"No. I didn't. So what did she do?"

"When she saw him? Nothing. She said he put his finger to his lips and asked her to keep quiet so he could slip out undetected."

"Then, of course, she called every reporter in Georgia," I say cynically, which makes him laugh. When he is done laughing, he shakes his head. "People. Huh? So, what's your favorite Elvis song?"

"Oh. I don't know. . . ."

"You don't know? Come on. You have to have a favorite Elvis song!"

"I like 'Suspicious Minds' a lot."

"Well, Ellie," he says, "you're in luck, because . . ." He reaches his hand under the seat and pulls out a box of cassettes.

"I think we have some of E's greatest hits on board. . . ." He begins fishing through the box. He asks the naked guy, "Hey, Mickey? Where's the Elvis Top 50?" Then he holds up his hand. "Never mind. Don't get up." He nudges me with his elbow and winks like it is our little joke on the naked guy. He holds up a tape. "Aha." He goes to the stereo and puts it in. "Are You Lonesome Tonight?" plays softly from the speakers. Aaron starts singing along. *"Are you lonesome tonight? Do you miss me tonight? Are you sorry we drifted apart? . . ."* He is off-key, but it is endearing.

He extends his hand. "Would you like to dance?"

Yes, but no. God, no.

"There's not really room," I say.

"Baloney." He pulls me up so that we are standing face-to-face in the aisle. He takes my hand in his and wraps his other hand on the small of my back. I only come to his chest. "There is always room for dancing," he says, and he moves me back and forth, swaying to the song. He sings again, *"Tell me dear, are you lonesome toniiiight? . . ."* His voice cracks and he starts laughing. "Don't quit your day job, right, Ratchett?"

"I thought it was good," I say.

"You're just being nice to me."

"No, really," I say. He stares at me for a long moment; it makes me need to look away, but he puts his hand on my face and makes me look at him. He smiles and says, "Well, aren't you the prettiest thing?"

He motions to the couch. "Will you sit with me a while?"

"Sure."

"Would you like some water?"

"Okay."

He goes to the tiny refrigerator and fishes out a bottle of Evian and twists open the cap. I'm so thirsty, I take big gulps. He puts his hand on mine. "Take your time," he says. When I am done, he takes the bottle and sets it on the table.

"Thank you."

He just nods, his eyes fixed on me. "You have very pretty eyes, Ellie. Has anyone ever told you that?" I shake my head no. I want to tell him how Gwen's are better, but I don't. I save this one for me. "Well, you do. They're like little emeralds. Your boyfriend is very lucky." I feel my face fall, the tug in my throat.

"I . . . I don't have a boyfriend," I say. He smiles and puts his arm around me.

"Well, then. Looks like *I'm* the lucky one." He takes my hand and squishes it between his fingertips. "You have the softest hands," he says. He motions to Naked Man. "Dude, you gotta feel these hands. They're like little paws."

"You're embarrassing me," I say. But it's not all true. It's a good embarrassed, anyway.

"You're cute when you're embarrassed." He leans in closer. "Can I kiss you, Ellie?"

Reflexively, I feel my body stiffen. He backs up. "It's okay," he says. I relax again. He presses my hand to his lips and kisses it. Quick, like a peck.

"There," he says. "I kissed you. Not so bad, huh?" I laugh, feeling silly. "Sorry," I say. "I'm not in a very happy mood."

"What's the matter?" he asks. I shrug my shoulders.

"Nothing. I'm just . . . I am upset over a guy. I thought he was the one . . . but he loves someone else."

He puts his hands on my face. "Oh, honey, I'm so sorry to hear that. What's his name, I'll have Mickey kick his ass for you."

"No. I don't want you to hurt him. I just . . . don't want to feel this way anymore."

He hugs me. "No. Of course you don't. And you know what they say? Don't you?"

"No. What?"

"The best way to get over a guy is to get under one."

He looks at my face, waiting for the reaction. It takes me a minute, then I get it, and my eyes widen. He cracks up laughing.

"I'm kidding! Jesus, you should have seen your face!"

I start laughing, relieved and embarrassed all at once. He laughs with me. "See?" he says. "That's better. You're much prettier when you smile. You have a dynamite smile, Ellie. God, how corny. *Dynamite smile.* That's such a '50s thing to say. But it's true. You could do toothpaste commercials."

"Really?"

"Absolutely. Have you ever thought about being an actress?"

I shake my head. "No."

"Well, you should. You've already got the name. What's your last name?"

"Roma."

He makes a motion with his hand like he is reading it on a marquee. "*Ellie Roma.* Yep. Sounds like a movie star to me."

I smile at him and he leans in a little closer. "I couldn't take my eyes off of you all night, Movie Star, did you know that? It was hard to concentrate."

"Really?"

"Really." He laughs too, then his face gets serious. "Come here."

All at once he pulls me to him and I feel his lips on mine. He presses into me, a long, soft kiss like I have only seen on TV. He pulls back and rests his forehead on mine. Nose to nose, he says, "Wow. You're a really great kisser."

Several months ago I read some tips in Celia's *Seventeen* magazine, and we practiced on her Simon Le Bon poster once. We didn't want to mess up John's face. That's why I'm so good, I guess. Celia said when you use tongues you should do a little swirl inside their mouth, like you are looking for a Tic Tac. But I've never tried that. I thought when I did it for real it would be Leo.

He takes my face in his hands and leans in, but he doesn't kiss me. Instead, he takes in a long, deep breath and I hear a low, satisfied moan. Even my smell is good, I guess. He gives me a small, tender kiss on my ear, and then he whispers just for me, "Do you want to come to the back and see my room?"

"Your room?"

"Yeah. It's really cool. I have a little TV with a VHS and everything. We could watch *Blue Hawaii*. It's way more comfortable than out here. . . ."

"Well, I'm waiting for my sister. I don't want her to think I left . . ."

Just then, as if on cue, we hear the sounds of girls giggling from the back of the bus. He waves his hand. "She's fine. Mickey will tell them where we are. Right Mick?"

Mickey is drinking the milk from his bowl and gives a thumbs-up.

"Well," I say, stalling, "you just put the cassette in . . ."

He reaches over and ejects the Elvis tape from the deck. "I have a stereo back there too, darlin'." He leans in and kisses me on the lips, slow and lingering. He runs his hand through my hair and smiles at me, expectantly but with sleepy eyes. "Ellie," he says, "are you a party girl like your big sister?"

"A party girl? Well, I suppose it depends on what you mean by 'party girl.' I mean, *define* 'party girl.' I've *been* to parties. I enjoy a festive atmosphere as much as the next guy. . . ."

Aaron shifts his weight on the couch; his irritation is palpable. He takes a deep breath and leans in even closer, probably so the naked guy won't hear. "Listen, sweetie," he says, "are we going to have sex or not?"

Well, my stomach just packed its bags and went diving.

"I don't . . . I've never done that before. And . . . I . . . I think you're really nice and everything, but . . ."

He pulls away. I feel him erect the invisible force field that now stands between us, like he'd pushed the button for the limo partition to rise and now I am on the other side, my nose pressed to the glass. His smile is long gone. I feel awful. No, worse: *punished.*

"Were you just playing games with me?" he asks.

"Me? No. I don't even know what that means. . . ."

"Don't play dumb. Sitting here flirting with me like some *tease.*"

I stammer, trying to make sense of it, wondering where the nice guy went, wondering what I did to make him leave, wondering what I can do to get him to come back.

"I'm sorry," I say. "I didn't mean to hurt your feelings. Believe me, I know how it feels. I think you're really sweet. Let's just . . . we could watch *Blue Hawaii* . . ."

"No. You know what? I'm really exhausted," he says. "We're driving to Detroit tonight, it's gonna be a long drive."

"Oh," I say. "Okay."

He stands up. "It was nice to meet you, Ellie."

"Well, you don't have to go. I mean, we could . . ."

Before I can finish, he has moved to the front of the bus and disappeared behind the curtain that separates the driver from the rest of the bus. I hear the sound of voices from up there, but I can't decipher the whispery sounds. Suddenly, a loud British voice booms from the front of the bus.

"Time to roll, everyone!" I look up to find a very fat bald man with a moustache emerging from behind the curtain. He is missing a good percentage of his teeth. "Let's go, everyone! Time to roll!" He walks past me to the back of the bus and bangs on the door. "Party's over, folks! Time to go!" He bangs again.

Suddenly, Justina and Gwen come crashing through the back door. They are laughing, loud, and smashed out of their brains.

"Ell! 'Sup, sister?" They stumble over each other as the British guy guides them to the front of the bus. "Ladies, right this way," and he begins to herd us toward the exit, grabbing Justina by the elbow. "Chill out, dude," she says, and jerks her arm away. I look back for Aaron. Over my shoulder I see him come out from behind the curtain. He walks right past me toward the back of the bus. I wave good-bye, but he just looks away like he has never seen me before. At first I feel the sting. But then, all at once, I see him for who he is, and in that realization I see my own reflection, that part of myself that I have seen before, the one my mother knows so well. The one that's as hopeful as it is unrealistic. That can't see good and bad at the same time.

The British guy booms his voice again, jolting me out of my head and back onto the bus. "Okay, everyone who is not going to Detroit needs to get off the bus. Now!"

"Jesus Christ. We heard you. Fucker," Gwen says, her voice showing the usual disdain.

"What did you say?"

I take her arm. "Nothing," I say. "It's fine. We're leaving." I take Gwen by the arm and lead her down the stairs. I can smell her breath from here. As soon as our feet find the gravel, the bus door closes behind us.

Justina kicks gravel at the door and turns back to us. "What the hell was that all about?"

Gwen commiserates. "I know. We were having a great time, hanging out with Ronnie and Steve, and suddenly Mr. Buzzkill comes a-knockin'."

"*Asshole,*" Justina says and shakes her head. I see them get the thought at the same time, and they both turn to me and shoot me the stink-eye.

"What?" I ask guiltily.

Gwen eyes me suspiciously. "What happened? What did you do?"

"Me? Nothing. I didn't do anything."

Justina takes a step toward me, nearly knocking me over with her Jack Daniels breath. "Did you just get us thrown off that bus?"

"Of course not! I can't believe you would even *say* that!"

They look at each other and nod. "Yep. I knew it. She got us kicked off the Kix tour bus."

"No, I didn't!"

They take a side bar, talk amongst themselves for a moment, then Justina says, "Of course, now we'll have to kill her."

Gwen agrees. "How should we do it?"

Justina looks at me. "*Torture.*"

"You guys! I kissed him, okay? And then . . . he wanted to have sex! And I just . . . couldn't." I look down, embarrassed. "I'm sorry. But . . . my heart belongs to someone else."

I look up and they are staring at me, like they aren't sure they'd heard me right.

Gwen cocks her head to one side. "He tried to fuck you?"

I nod. "I think so."

"And you just kissed him, right?" Gwen searches my face to be sure. Again, I nod. There is a long pause, then Justina says, "*Nice.* Was that your first kiss?"

"Unless you count the time Herbie Szymanski planted one

on me in first grade while we were square dancing . . . yes. It was my first kiss."

Justina places a hand over her heart. "My little Ellie's all growed up."

"Very funny. I'm glad you're amused."

"I'm just fucking with you, dude. You should be proud of yourself. Ratchett? For your first kiss? Not bad. Did he slip you the tongue?"

I shrug and look away. I try to hide it, but they see my face fall.

"What's wrong?" Justina asks.

"Nothing," I say, lying.

Gwen brings her up to speed. "We saw Leo. You know . . . the guy she likes. He was with someone else."

"Ouch." Justina places a hand on me sympathetically.

I nod my head, recalling the torment. "She's a *woman*," I say.

"Well," she says, "you know what that means, dude. You gotta fight fire with fire."

"What do you mean?"

"Get him into bed and he's yours."

Gwen hits her on the arm. "What the hell is wrong with you?" she says. "Just because *you* got on your back for a promotion at the Hair Cuttery." She looks at me. "Justina is now *head* shampoo girl. She thinks her shit doesn't stink."

"Fuck off. I'm just giving the girl advice," Justina rubs her arm.

"Well, *don't*."

They start to get into it, their voices escalating in a drunken frenzy.

"You guys!" I say, suddenly myself again. "Listen. I hate to interrupt, but we have to go. Mom's gonna be home in like half an hour."

Justina gathers herself and fishes for her car keys. "Okay . . . okay . . . where's the car?" she says, dazed, and lets out a huge belch, sending them both into hysterical laughter.

"Who can drive?" Gwen and Justina just look at each other and start laughing again.

"Shit. Gwen, if Mom gets home before we do, we're screwed."

Gwen puts her hand up to me. "Chill out."

"Chill out? How are we supposed to get home?"

"Don't worry," she says. "I'll drive."

"You're worse than she is. *Shit.*"

Justina wobbles toward me. "Everybody relax," she says, her words oozing out of her mouth. "Ellie, you get us to Rockshire and I can go the rest of the way to my house."

"Me? Justina. I don't drive."

"Well, now you'll learn."

I rub my face, smearing my makeup. "Jesus Christ."

We climb into the car, everyone in front at first, and then Justina climbs over the seat to get in the back, which, for some reason is the funniest thing either of them have ever seen. I lift my butt up and remove the phone book, which, again, causes them to erupt in laughter again. For my part, I am like the person at the scene of an accident, lining up the victims for triage, my brain focused on the matter at hand.

I put the keys in the ignition and the car groans to life. "Now what?"

Justina leans over from the backseat. "Sometimes the reverse doesn't work so good. Don't back out. Just go around."

"This car's a piece of junk," Gwen offers.

I give it a little gas, too much, and the car lurches forward. "We're gonna die!" they scream, and the laughing starts all over again. All the spit has left my mouth. I steer the car out of the parking lot and begin searching for the entrance to I-95. I take it inch by inch, one thing at a time. My thoughts begin to organize themselves. Burn victims are more urgent than broken bones, internal injuries more pressing than flesh wounds. Ah . . . but then how do you assess internal injuries? I shake my head to clear it out, make myself think, *Just stay between the lines.*

"Where do I go?"

"Just straight."

"I know. After that."

"Get off at Seneca Highway. You know it from there, right?"

"I think so."

I look at the clock on the dash. We have twenty minutes until our mom is supposed to be home, but I don't want to go any faster. Fifty feels like flying.

"Why is everyone so serious?" Gwen turns on the radio. Whitesnake is on. She tosses her hair around and sings along: *"In the still of the night I hear the wolf howl honey sneakin' around your door. . . ."* Justina answers back with the next line, *"In the still of the night I feel my heart feel heavy tellin' me you gotta have moooore! . . ."* Then they both go, *"Oooohhh baby!"*

Gwen puts her hand on my arm. "Sing with us, Ellie." But I am frozen still, because I just noticed that beside me on the left is a cop. I turn the radio off. Gwen turns to yell at me, but then she sees it too.

"Fuck," she says.

I hear Justina from the backseat. "Be cool, y'all."

We all face front, our heartbeats the only sound we make. The cop rides alongside us for nearly a mile. I don't breathe. *Stay in the lines, Ellie. Just stay in the lines.*

"Seneca Highway is just ahead," Justina says, her lips barely moving. "Start getting over now." I begin to steer the car toward the right. "Blinker!" she yells. "Use your blinker!"

"Which one's that?"

"On the left. Put it up."

I reach my hand over like she says, but the windshield wipers start going. "The *other* one!"

"Shit!" I start shaking, and then I feel the tears coming. I cannot do this. What was I thinking? Just then the lights on top of the cop car start to flash, the red and blue illuminating our faces. I look at Gwen, my pulse throbbing through my whole body. "I'm sorry," I say. But then, all of a sudden, there are no more lights on her face. I look over and the cop has sped away. I see his lights flashing ahead of us, watch his taillights disappear up the highway.

"Oh, my God," I say.

Justina clutches her chest and throws herself on the backseat. "My freakin' *heart*," she says.

"I need a smoke." Gwen lights a cigarette, takes a drag, and offers it to me. I actually hold my hand out to take it; that's when I notice the trembling. Instead, I shake my head no.

I move the car to the shoulder and stop. I find the *P* on the gearshift and collapse over the steering wheel. Gwen puts her hand on my thigh. "See how good you are?" she says. "I knew you'd know what to do." She's reaching to turn the radio back on when she notices I'm shaking.

"Ellie? Are you okay?"

I nod my head yes.

She leans in. "You did the right thing tonight. With Ratchett." I just nod. "You did. You always do. You're so grounded and together." I shake my head and look away. "What?" she asks.

Well, I'd rather be flying and falling apart. But there is no one to catch me, no one to put me back together.

"Nothing," I say.

Justina pipes in from the backseat, "I hate to ruin this hallmark moment, but Cinderella's gonna turn into a pumpkin if we don't get back before the evil stepmother does." We turn around and look at her. "Or am I confusing fairy tales?"

I shake my head and put the car in drive like I know how to do now. I use the turn signal and get off at Seneca Highway. Then I follow my memory until it leads us home.

thirteen

once we are off the highway, I am much more relaxed. As we approach our neighborhood, I steady the car and make a wide turn onto our street and cut off the engine. Her car is not out front. "She's not home," I say. "Hurry."

Gwen and I get out and walk the rest of the way. Gwen is stumbling now and again; I try to hold her up, try to keep her straight and quiet. It feels familiar, like what I am always trying to do with her.

We cut across the common lawn and I see Leo's van parked outside his house. I am leading Gwen to the back of the house when I see him, leaning against the van, smoking a cigarette.

"Hey! There's Leo!" she slurs, grabbing my arm and leading me over.

"Hey," he says.

"Hi." I begin working the pavement with the toe of Gwen's turquoise scrunch boot.

"Did you guys have fun?"

Gwen flails an arm, her movements sloppy and sudden. "We had a fucking blast, man." Then she says, remembering, "You know, your girlfriend's a bitch."

Leo shakes his head. "I'm, uh . . . I'm sorry about that." He looks at me. "And she's not my girlfriend." Do I hear angels? The heavens parting? I pause, wait for doves to swoop down and tie bows in my hair.

"Oh," I say. "I didn't know."

"She can be mean. I'm sorry if she hurt your feelings." He looks me over. "You look pretty, Ellie. But . . . you don't need all of that."

I pull up the top of the tube dress.

"We gotta go," Gwen reminds me.

"Sorry. My mom will be home any second."

He nods. "Okay."

"Okay," I say reluctantly. "Good night."

I lead Gwen around back and feel around for the window. I slide it open. Gwen climbs in first, then me. It's hard in the dress, but I wiggle my way over the sill headfirst and catch myself on the other side, my hands on the carpet.

The house is dark; I feel around for the light switch. Gwen leans on me as we begin to make our way upstairs.

I hear my mom's car pull up out front. We get up to Gwen's room and begin pulling her clothes off; her shorts get stuck around her cowboy boots and she face-plants into the carpet. I pick her up and pull the boots off. I pull off my tube dress and lift the covers.

"Get in." She slides under and I run to my bedroom, slip into my Care Bear pajamas. I hear Mom's key in the door. I run back to Gwen's room. She's still wearing the gloves. I go over and pull them off, stuff them under the bed.

"Gwen. Don't get up. Okay? Be asleep." I close her door and go into the bathroom. I get a hot washcloth and wipe off my face, brush my hair out. When I come out of the bathroom, she is still downstairs. I walk toward my room. . . .

"Who's that?" she calls up.

I back up, go to the landing. "It's just me, Mommy. How was your date?"

"Ellie. Please stop yelling. Come down here if you want to talk."

I pack on my armor and plod slowly down the stairs and toward the kitchen. I stand in the entryway, careful not to cross the threshold. She is hunched over the sink in the dark, spreading peanut butter on Saltines.

"I just said, how was your date?"

She swallows her cracker, fixes her mouth to answer me, then stops. She cocks her head to the side, squints a little.

"What's all over your face?"

"Oh." I bring my hand to my face. "We were playing dress-up."

"Where's Gwen?"

"Sleeping."

Upstairs there is a thud. I hear Gwen's door open.

"She's up *now*," she says. I nod, smile. "Probably has to

pee," I say. She takes another bite of cracker but keeps her eyes on me, looking for a way to see in. I shuffle my feet nervously.

"It's weird to see you eat," I say.

"What's that supposed to mean?"

"No, nothing. You just . . . well . . . I mean, that's how you stay so slim, I guess! Me, I could just eat and eat and eat. . . ." I hear the bathroom door open upstairs. My heart leaps up into my throat, starts throbbing.

"Are you okay?" she asks.

"Me? Oh . . . I'm just tired." I stretch my arms overhead and yawn. "Pooped." And then I hear them. Gwen's footsteps on the stairs.

"Welp, that's it for me. I'll see you tomorrow." I whip myself around to go stop Gwen on the stairs, but when I get there, she is already on the second landing, wearing nothing but black underwear, that black bustier, and all of that hair.

"I'm hungry," she says. I can smell her breath, yeasty and warm.

In my lowest voice I say, "Come upstairs with me. Okay?" I take her by the elbow but she yanks it away, "No. I'm hungry."

"Gwen," I say, my eyes pleading, "I'll bring you food, okay? I'll bring you peanut butter and crackers. How's that?" I try to take her arm again but she pulls away and goes down the stairs.

I try to stop her, but she stumbles right into the kitchen. I hear my mother say something about her outfit, but Gwen ignores it, opens the refrigerator door, slams it shut. "Nothing." She looks over at my mother, now replacing the twist tie on the Saltines and returning them to the cupboard.

"Do you mind sharing?" she says, holding out her hand. Now I am like the other type of person at the scene of an accident, the one who stops and watches, helpless but unable to look away. Just standing by, waiting to see how bad it is.

My mother pushes the Saltines toward her. Gwen unties the bag of crackers and asks for the peanut butter, her movements slow and deliberate as she spreads it on a cracker. My mother watches her with unusual interest, then she stops as though something has interrupted her. She takes a step toward Gwen.

"Have you been drinking?"

Gwen laughs. "Have *you*?"

My mother grabs her by the chin.

"Mom, please, leave her alone." I say. "Let's just go to bed."

"I told you not to leave this house. Didn't I?" Gwen looks away. "Didn't I? Answer me!"

"Yes."

"Then do you mind telling me what in the hell you were doing?"

"I was getting food," she says, crumbs falling from her mouth.

My mother turns to me. "Did you know about this?" I shake my head no, but then she grabs me by the hair. "Don't lie to me!"

"Let go of her!" Gwen screams and pushes my mother away, nearly knocking her to the floor.

"You are going to jail," she says. "I've had it with you."

"Good. Call the cops. Jail would be better than here! I hate you!"

My mother's hand whips across Gwen's face and the slapping sound reverberates in my bones.

"Don't you ever say that to me. You hear me?"

Gwen stands there for a moment, stunned, her hand held to her ear where most of the impact was. That one hurt. And then, in seemingly slow motion, she raises her hand and, my God, she slaps my mother back.

I watch my mother's face register what just happened. First confusion, then embarrassment, then rage unleashed. In a sudden explosion she comes at Gwen from all sides; with her entire body she starts smacking and punching and pulling at Gwen, who to my amazement does not back down. She is punching too and grabbing at my mother's hair, but it is too short for a good hold. Within seconds, they are on the floor, my mother straddling her, her hands around Gwen's neck.

Gwen starts kicking her legs wildly, pushes her palm into my mother's face, trying to dislodge her.

I stand helplessly to the side, frozen, as Gwen's kicking begins to weaken. She makes a horrible, tight-sounding wail as she gasps for air and tries to pull my mother's hands away from her throat. But my mother is all determination.

"Mom! Stop it!" Finally my voice returns. I run over, try to shake her, try to bring her back from wherever she has gone. She lets go and slides off of Gwen and onto the floor. Gwen crawls to the far wall, gulping for air. The three of us sit in silence, unsure of what to do next. Finally, my mother picks herself up from the floor.

"Are you okay?" Gwen rubs her throat, nods her head.

"Then you get upstairs and sleep it off." She turns to go. I look at Gwen, who's still struggling for air.

"That's it?" I say. "You almost kill her, and that's it?"

My mother turns back around in slow motion and stares at me. "You got something to say to me?"

"No, ma'am."

She crosses her arms, satisfied. "I didn't think so."

We lock eyes for a moment, then she breaks the contact. "Well," she says. "I think I've had enough for one evening." She turns to go, but before she does she says, with true sadness, "I don't know what I did to deserve such hateful children."

She goes upstairs and I hear her bedroom door close. I stay behind with Gwen, wait for her breathing to return to normal. I don't say anything to her because nothing I could say would undo this and nothing else is worth saying.

She goes up to her room and I go to mine. After a few minutes, I hear noises from her room, so I get up and go to her door. I enter uninvited and close the door behind me. She is standing beside her bed, arms full of clothes. She looks up, startled.

"Jesus," she says. "I thought you were Mom."

Her green Britches duffel bag, which I know she hates because she says it's "too preppy," is open on the bed. She stuffs an armful of clothes into it.

"What are you doing?" I ask, whispering.

"I'm leaving," she says.

"Where are you going?"

"I'm not telling you. You'll tell Mom."

I put my hand up. "I won't. I swear."

"It doesn't matter where I'm going. Just that it's not here."

"Can I come?"

"No."

"Why not?"

"Ellie. Stop. This isn't a game."

"What are you going to do for money?"

"I'll be fine. Justina's sister lives in New York, she works at a club, and she's gonna get us jobs." She points her finger at me. "Don't tell."

"I *won't*. But . . . you have to be eighteen to serve alcohol."

"Do you?" She shrugs. "Then we'll strip."

"Gwen!"

"Ssshhh. Keep your voice down. It's not forever. Just until we get enough money to start our band."

"You don't even play an instrument."

"Well, then I'll learn."

She grabs Jimmy Bear, he looking as surprised as ever, and puts him in the bag.

"This doesn't sound like a very good plan."

"Well, it's all I got."

"Why don't you sleep on it? Think about it in the morning when you're good and sober."

"I'm not *drunk,* Ellie. I know what I'm doing. I am sick of her, I am sick of this place, and I am getting the hell out of here."

"But . . . what about me?"

"You'll be fine. Things will be a lot better around here without me."

"Or worse."

"You know how to handle her. You never get it as bad as I do."

She zips up her bag and takes a deep breath and looks at me, serious. "Don't rat me out," she says.

I don't say anything. I'm not really sure what to do. Part of me wants to stop her, to go get my mom and somehow make her stay, *something*. But there is this other part of me saying, *Go, Gwen. Just go.* It isn't that I won't miss her, because I will. It's just that I've missed her for so long already. Even when she was here, she wasn't.

She puts the duffel bag over her shoulder and holds her finger to her lips, and I watch her creep out the door and disappear down the stairs. I hold my breath, hear the door open and close. Then I hear the sound of footsteps fading up the sidewalk.

I stand alone in her room, feel the weight of how it is just me here now. I absentmindedly take a few turns of her Rubik's Cube. She's solved two colors; I change them to a checkerboard. An act previously forbidden. I shake her snow globe of Busch Gardens, watch as the flurry of glitter surrounds the tiny Clydesdale horses before settling back on the bottom. None of it provides the thrill I thought it would.

I go into my room and stretch out on my bed, but something is different. I can't seem to crawl inside my head. Instead, I have the urge to *do* something. It's kind of like that feeling when you solve a riddle, that *Why didn't I see this before?* feeling. You can't just sit there and keep trying to solve it, you have to get up and get on with things.

My adrenaline pumping, I take my school backpack from

underneath my bed and begin stuffing clothes into it. I even remember underwear and a toothbrush, which shows I have presence of mind even though I feel like I am on autopilot. I tiptoe past my mother's room, listen for her slow and heavy breathing.

As quietly as humanly possible, I creep down the stairs, avoiding the one that squeaks. I open the front door and step outside into the familiar soupy air of a summer evening, raise my arm up so the gnats won't fly into my eyes. I put one foot in front of the other until I am at Leo's front door. Trembling, I knock softly. Here we go.

He opens the door, and immediately his eyebrows scrunch together in concern.

"Ellie?"

I nod but cannot form words.

"Come in."

He takes a step back to allow me in the door. The inside of his house smells like burnt toast, and it undoes me. I collapse onto his chest and hold on for dear life. I can feel tears deep inside me, but they won't fill my eyes. I can't let go, I just hang on in silence. Finally Leo takes me by the shoulders and pulls me back away from him.

"What happened?" he says. "Are you okay?"

"Yes," I say. *I am now.*

fourteen

Leo leads me down the stairs to the basement, where his bedroom is. His mattress is on the floor; a bare lightbulb hangs from directly above it. Hardly the honeymoon suite I had envisioned. But life is about improvising, right? I can see us here, though, sparse as it is. Him coming home late from rehearsal, me reading my book in my nightgown. Waiting for him, but not hovering. "How was practice?" I will ask. "It was okay." But his voice will be thick with something and I will sense it without him having to say. I will tell him, "I believe in you. You are so talented." And then his whole body will soften and he will crawl into bed and thank me with his kisses.

I will have to meet his parents, since we will probably be living together for a while, at least until Leo and I get our own place. And then it will just be the two of us, and our new privacy will make the whole relationship feel new. We will carry on through the intimacy of everyday life on new feet, relishing in the little discoveries we make about each other. "Why, I didn't know you loved *olives.*" And then I will make something with olives in it, just whip it up out of nowhere, a napkin folded neatly beside the plate.

I sit down on the corner of his bed and look around the room. There is one window, which is at ground level, and it smells like it had rained on the carpet. I notice cardboard boxes strewn across the room; most of them are open but still full. I look in the box right beside me; it is full of albums. I pull them out one by one. AC/DC. Aerosmith. The Beatles. All in alphabetical order.

"Everything's still in boxes. It's like you never unpacked."

"Actually, I'm packing up."

"What for?" Maybe his parents are planning a remodel. Everyone should have a finished basement.

"I'm leaving."

A trip. Well, I hadn't expected this, but again, improvisation and compromise are the cornerstones of a good relationship.

"Where are you going?"

"Los Angeles."

"California? For how long?"

Leo stops and looks at me. "For good."

The sledgehammer. Crushing at my insides. Again. This guy is the Mike Tyson of emotional sucker punches.

"But why?"

"Because there's nothing for me here. And the longer I stay, the more afraid I become."

"Of what?"

"Of never becoming anything. Of becoming one of those people who only talk about their dream and never do anything about it."

"Is the band going with you?"

"No. Just Eddie. His brother's out there already. He says he can hook us up with his buddies and maybe get us some gigs on the Strip."

"What about Tina? He's just going to leave her here?"

"No. She's coming too. As soon as she's done with nursing school."

"Tina's a *nurse*?" I say, a little too loudly I think, because he pauses and looks at me. "Are you all right?"

"I . . . when are you leaving?"

"Tonight."

He gets up from the bed and starts taping up a box. He rips the tape off with his teeth, and there is such a sense of determination in him when he does it that it allows for some momentary bravery in me.

I can't look at him, so I keep my eyes to the floor and listen as the words march out of my mouth. "Leo?" I hear myself say. "Can I come to California with you?"

Leo's expression is one of utter confusion, like he isn't sure he heard me right. He repeats my question back to me instead of answering it.

"Can you come to California with me?"

"Yes."

"Why would you want to do that?"

"I don't want to just talk about my dreams either."

"But what would you *do* out there?"

"Write. I told you, remember?"

"But you have to graduate before you can be a writer, and probably go to college, too."

"Well, then I could hang out with you. In your free time, I mean. Because I know you'll be really busy and everything. But I could be a big help with that. I'm very organized."

"You wouldn't want to do that."

"Sure I would!"

"I don't think that's such a good idea."

"Why?"

"I'll get arrested, for one. How old are you?"

"Technically?"

"As opposed to what? *Yes,* technically."

"Well, *technically* I'm fourteen . . . but there is a thirty-five-year-old in me just dying to get out."

He stifles a laugh. "Well . . . that's a bit of a problem, don't you think?"

"No. There are ways around it."

"Like?"

"I don't know. I haven't thought it through yet. You just sprang this on me at the last minute."

"Listen. I know things are tough, Ellie. And I'm flattered. I really am. But . . ."

"Don't say no, Leo. Please don't say no."

Leo takes a step toward me, reaches out for me, but I don't like what his face is saying. "Listen, Ellie . . ."

"No. *You* listen. I love you, okay? I love you so much it hurts. My whole insides ache. I can't take it."

"What? No, Ellie, you don't love me."

"Don't say that! Please don't say that. I *do*. I'll show you. . . ." I stand up and face him. I begin to undo the buttons on my blouse.

"No . . ."

"Yes. Please. Leo, I want to show you. I know you think I'm a little girl, but I'm not. I'm old inside. And I *love* you." I continue undoing my top, then the button on my jeans. "Let me."

"Stop."

"Why? Am I so awful?"

"No. It's just . . . you don't want it to happen like this."

"The other night after band practice you were going to kiss me, I could tell. And I just got all nervous because I'd never kissed a boy before, but we could do it now. . . ."

He takes me by the shoulders, his face so tender.

"Ellie. You're going to love someone for real, I promise. You're fourteen. You're not even formed. You can be anything you want. You don't want me."

"You're wrong, Leo. I—"

"Listen to me. You're bright and funny. . . ."

"Then take me with you. Please. Just love me. Is that so hard?"

"It doesn't work like that."

"Then how does it work? Huh? Show me! I don't understand."

"Ellie, listen . . ."

Here come the tears, ugly, the chin wiggle and everything.

"Why were you so nice to me? You just let me hope! And it isn't fair, because now you're taking everything away. You won't let me have any of it. I hate you!"

I collapse into a heap on the floor, feel the despair pour out of me from my darkest corners. The tears come so fast I begin to choke on them. I wipe my face on my shirtsleeve, but when I do, I pull a long string of snot away with it. Leo reaches into a box and hands me a roll of pink toilet paper. Reluctantly, I say thank you and turn my head away from him as I blow my nose. When I finally gather myself I say, "You really won't take me to California?"

Leo smoothes my hair and, with tenderness all over his face, he says, "No, sweetie. I won't."

"I'll bet you'll date Playboy Centerfolds, huh?" The vision: Leo in his pajamas like Hugh Hefner, flanked by two blondes with tight, shiny bodies. I hadn't even thought of that until now. How could I have been so stupid?

The worst part is that underneath the humiliation is the feeling I've done something wrong. Like, if I had done or said something different or if I looked different, that he would want me to go. My mind races backward; flashes of my naïveté and adolescent awkwardness scream out to me. God, and my *outfits*. The tube dress. Those tight overall shorts. What was I thinking? My big ass all over the place. I should have done more cardio. Snacked less. Small things, but they would have added up. I see that now.

"I guess you must think I'm pretty stupid."

"I don't think you're stupid."

"It doesn't mean I don't love you, though."

He smiles at me, but it is a tiny smile. Everything he does right now is small, all of his movements. He is being so careful with me, like he thinks I might break.

"Let's get some air, okay?"

We go out the front door and sit on his stoop. I look at my house across the street from a different perspective. The first firefly flashes right next to me, catching me off guard. I am startled, and then I smile before my brain can remind me I am sad.

Leo pulls a cigarette from the pack. Around us, the fireflies are blinking wildly, on and off in a nearly syncopated rhythm.

"Look at that," he says. "They're almost in synch. And they're flashing green."

"Mating call."

"Really? How'd you know that?"

I look at the sidewalk, study the cracks in the pavement. "My father told me."

In my peripheral vision, I see Leo's face change. His words take a gentle step toward me.

"Your dad, huh? Where's he at?"

I don't really answer him. I shrug off the question and let it fall to the ground below. But Leo picks it up and continues.

"Do you miss him?" His question touches a place that is deep within me, a place that has its own twenty-four-hour guard with a hat and a uniform and everything. I rake my hand through my hair to postpone the emotion that is welling up in me.

"Yes," I say finally, my voice so small.

Just then a firefly lands on my knee. I look at it up close.

"It's a female," I say.

"How do you know?"

"The red stripe. See?"

Leo leans closer to it. "Look at that. I never noticed that. Did you ever catch them?" I shake my head no. "I did. I would put them in a jar and keep them for a little while. Never overnight, though. I knew this kid who kept them in a jar overnight once. When he woke up, they'd all died, even though he'd poked holes in the lid."

"That's a good way to analyze people. Like that inkblot test."

"Yeah. Let's see. There's the people like *you,* who just want to watch them and be close to them."

"And there's the people like *you,* who just want to hold them for a little while. . . ."

"And there's the people like that kid I knew, who just can't leave well enough alone. Who have to hold on to something so long that they hurt it."

I look up at my house, its cold, gray stoop. I see her car out front. From here I can see the pool of oil that has gathered on the pavement beneath it.

"And then," I say, without taking my eyes off my house, "there are the people who step on them and drag their foot along the sidewalk, squishing all the light out of them."

He puts his cigarette out in the grass. Out of the corner of my eye I see him scan my face for a moment, then pick at a scab on his elbow. The cicadas throb in unison, keeping perfect time. He looks at me, serious.

"There will always be people in life that want what you've got, Ellie."

I hesitate. "Okay."

"Really. I want to tell you this. That thing you think is out there somewhere, the thing you think is in me? It's in you, too. Do you understand?"

I nod. "I think so."

He looks at me. "You've already got it. Okay?"

"Okay."

"You have to protect it." His eyes search my face and he looks away, frustrated. "Maybe you'll understand one day."

"No," I say. "No, I think I do."

"Okay."

"This life stuff is hard, huh?"

He laughs softly. "Yes," he says, "I guess it is." He looks up at my house. "Do you know what you're going to do?"

I bite down on my top lip and shake my head, roll a blade of grass between my fingers. "Is there anyone you can call?" I think about Celia's mom, but that wouldn't work in the long run. Besides, I'm not ready to tell anyone about this.

"What about your dad? Can you call him?" I shake my head no. "You can't call your dad?"

Not only do I not respond, I don't even look up. I would have, but I've found a small patch of dirt and am suddenly very busy digging into it with my finger.

"Ellie?"

I'm thinking I'll just keep digging until I get somewhere. China, maybe. That would be good. Maybe a little Chinaman will stick his head out of the ground, Peking hat and all, and invite me to tea. I'll have Lapsang souchong or Jasmine Pearl—something exotic. I bet he'll use the good china. I wonder if they call it china when you're *in* China.

"Did you hear me?"

I finally look up.

"Yes," I say, "I heard you."

"Then tell me. Why can't you call your dad?"

"Be*cause*. I just can't, okay?"

"Did he ever do anything bad to you?"

"He left."

"Okay. But you saw him after that, right?"

"Yes. At first."

"So what happened?"

"I don't know. It just got too hard. Every time we went to his house our mom acted like we were abandoning her or something. It was like we had to pick sides and it was just easier . . . not to. Besides, she needs me more than he does. And it's not all bad. She tries really hard sometimes."

He turns and looks at me, his face so serious. "Ellie," he says, "you can't fix her."

"I *know*."

"Do you?"

"Look. I know what I'm doing. And as for my dad, I think he just wants to start over. He doesn't need me as some reminder of the life he hated. I don't want to be that."

"Maybe you're not that."

"And maybe I am. Trust me. It's better this way."

"Why?"

"Because, what if it's true? At least now I have the hope."

"Ellie. You can't live on hope."

"I'm doing okay so far. Look, I really appreciate what you're trying to do. But it just . . . is what it is. Okay? I'm sorry, but . . . it's not your problem to solve."

Leo puts one hand up in a minisurrender. "No," he says. "It isn't. This one is up to you. That is true." He pauses a moment. "Just do me one favor, will you?"

"What?"

"Tell me a story about your dad. Just one story that you can remember. Will you do that?"

I pick a dandelion from the lawn and am about to pop the top off when I notice a ladybug crawling on it. I find another dandelion nearby and transfer the ladybug to it, then watch as she circles happily. In my mind, I begin fishing around, looking for things. What I'm looking for, I'm not quite sure. My father feels so far away in my mind, locked behind a door I'm afraid to open, trapped under glass I'm not strong enough to break.

"Okay," I say finally. "I've got one."

Leo lights another cigarette, ready.

"I changed my name when I was six." Leo searches my face for where I am going. I begin talking fast as I remember. "When I was born, my parents named me Gabrielle, but everyone started calling me Gabby and I hated it. Then one day I went to see Gwen's ballet recital. They were dancing to that song 'Ellie the Elf.' You know that one? *'Ellie the Elf. Sittin' on a shelf.'* Anyway, I knew right then and there, that was the name for me. There was resistance to the name change of course. My mother took it personally, and I remember a neighbor accused me of being uppity."

Leo just stares at me, waiting for the punch line. "This is supposed to be about your dad. Remember?"

"It *is*. That's what I'm saying. In the end . . . it was my father who rallied to my side. He said, 'It's *her* name, for Christ's sake! Let her be called what she wants.'"

Leo smiles just a little bit; he seems pleased in some small way. "And so," he says, "you came to be called Ellie."

"And so I did."

There is a pause while this newness settles around us. Leo finishes his cigarette, and I feel our end coming too. I try to imprint his face in my mind so I won't ever forget it. I want everything to stay in me . . . his eyes, his cheeks, his lips, his hands. But somehow, I know they always will.

"I'll never forget you, Leo."

He hugs me and I bury my nose in his neck, try to take in the last remnants of his smell; already he smells warm and familiar—like a memory.

"Or I you, Ellie."

"And who knows," I say as he lets go, "ten years from now, a six-year age difference may seem like *nothing*. Especially if I become hot."

He laughs in spite of himself, and then, with a look that I will remember for the rest of my life, he says, "You're going to be amazing, Ellie. You already are."

We stand up and he hands me my backpack.

"Good-bye, Leo."

"See ya round, kid."

FiFteen

I walk back into my house and close the door softly behind me. I am about to head up the stairs when I notice my mother sitting on the sofa.

"Hey," she says. She is wearing her pink housecoat. The one with the zip. I put my backpack down on the steps and head for the living room.

"Hey," I say.

"Where've you been?" she asks without missing a beat.

I shake my head, remembering. "Nowhere."

She cranes her head, looking behind me. "Where's your sister?"

I pause for a moment. Deep breath. "Gone," I say.

She squints, not sure she heard me right. "What do you mean, *gone.*"

"Gone, as in not here, as in . . . she ran away."

"What?" Her voice trembles slightly. "Did you call Justina's?"

"Me? Did *I* call Justina's? No, I didn't call Justina's."

She stands up, becoming somewhat frantic, or at least pretending to, and disappears into the kitchen. I hear her pick up the phone, dial. Long pause, then she slams it back down. "Damn it!" She comes back into the living room.

"No answer." Then she starts throwing orders at me like darts. "Call Greg."

"It's three o'clock in the morning."

"Your sister has run away, Ellie! Call Celia, too."

"Mom, Celia's at camp."

"Jesus. I better call the police." She disappears up the stairs and I hear her on the phone. "Yes, I need to file a missing person's report . . . I *am* calm, damn it! . . . Um, a few hours, I think . . . what? She could be dead by then! Hello? . . . Hel-*lo*?" She slams the phone down. She pounds back down the stairs. "Useless!" She sees me in the living room, still standing where she left me. "I don't believe this." She points her finger at me. "You girls get away with too much! Do you see the state of me? These constant crises with you two."

I roll my eyes. *Oh, brother.*

"You know what?" She continues working herself up. "If she wants to run away, *fine.* It'll do her good. Let her get a taste of life on her own for a while. No one to clean up her messes. No one to save her from herself. She'll screw up and then she'll come crawling back here. You watch."

My normal procedure in this situation would be to stay quiet and under the radar until she has worn herself out. But this time, I hear myself say, "I hope not," and my voice is soft, because I don't have the flair for drama that Gwen does. Nor the appetite.

"What did you say?"

My courage wrests itself away from the rest of me and takes a small but deliberate step forward.

"I *said*, I hope she doesn't come back. I mean, why would you want her to?"

"Because she's my daughter."

"Really? Your daughter? What exactly does that mean to you, Mom?"

"You better watch yourself, girl."

"Or what? What are you gonna do? Hit me? And if Gwen comes back, you can smack her, too. Maybe you can *choke* her, then she can run off again, and you can run after her and get her to come back and then we can do it all over again. Doesn't that sound like fun?"

"Who do you think you're talking to? You're going to be like her now? You're the good one, Ellie. I don't need this shit from you."

"Good? Do you even see me? Do you even know who I am? I'm not good, Mom. And Gwen's not bad. We're just kids. *Your* kids."

"I've had enough of your mouth." She turns and begins to walk away.

"Why won't you listen? Everybody's leaving you, and you won't even listen. Our whole family is gone. . . ."

She turns back around. "Don't tell me about this family, Ellie. Your father is the one who walked out. . . ."

"But *why*? Why did he leave?"

"Because he's a no-good son-of-a-bitch, that's why! All he cares about is himself."

"But you're so mad all the time . . ."

"Don't you go putting this on me. He's a selfish bastard who walked out on you, and don't you ever forget it. He doesn't care about anyone but himself. He's a man, and that's how men *are*."

"No," I say. "Not all of them."

I realize what I have done too late. My heart stops and my face reveals me. She cranes her neck up and strokes her throat with the tip of her nail. A delighted Grinch-like smirk creeps onto her face. "You mean that little dirtbag across the street?" She begins to laugh. "Look at you. Some boy wants to stick his dick in you and you think you're all high-and-mighty."

"It's not like that!"

"Oh, please. Just don't come crying to me when he uses you up and throws you away, because I don't want to hear it."

And then suddenly, there it is. Placed right in my lap like a gift. And I think I know who put it there. *If she is wrong about that, then maybe she is wrong about a lot of things.* Like what I'm worth, for one.

I stare at her for a moment, then I walk to the stairs and pick up my backpack.

"Where are you going?"

I look at her, standing there in the living room like so many times before, but her tiny size is suddenly obvious to me. She's like one of those little dogs at the park who puff up the fur on their backs to seem bigger and more menacing to the other dogs, just in case one of them should try and start something. It's a defensive posture, meant to protect rather than incite. I'd never thought of that before.

"I'm leaving."

"Don't be so dramatic. Your father doesn't care about you, Ellie. Neither does that boy. I'm all you got, so just get used to it. Now, put your bag down."

"Is that why you're so mean? Because you're all we've got?" I stare at her and feel my eyes start to fill. "I just want to be happy. I want us to be a family. Please, Mom. For the last time. Why can't you be like other mothers? Why do you have to make it so hard? It doesn't have to be like this!"

For a moment, I think she will crack, that a sliver of light may have penetrated her veneer and she will break open, allowing me inside. But she pulls herself back together and points her finger in my face. "Let me tell you something, Ellie," she says. "You're not shit. So don't you be telling me about what I am."

It was the only hope I had allowed myself to have about her since I can remember. I feel my heart shatter into tiny fractals, feel them scatter through my body, the pain sharp and steady. A voice says to me, *This is all this will ever be,* and I feel some part of me, maybe just the part that doesn't have to study hard for vocab, but I feel something in me straighten itself and rise tall.

"You know what, Mommy?" I say. "Maybe I'm not shit. And maybe nobody will ever love me. But anything is better than this."

I throw my backpack over my shoulder and run for the front

door. She calls after me, "If you leave here, you are dead to me. Do you understand? I am not your mother."

I am gripped by a fear that is primal, the baby wolf cub straying too far from the cave. But I continue running toward the door because somewhere way in the back, behind my feeling of terror, is something that feels like the deepest relief.

"You're never going to let me love you, Mommy. And I'm tired of trying."

Then I turn the knob, take a breath, close my eyes . . . and I jump.

From his kitchen window I watch Leo as he loads the last box into the van. He is all flexed and sweaty from the heavy lifting. He calls in to me.

"You ready?"

I come outside and he points at my backpack with his chin. "Is that it?"

"Yes," I say. "This is it."

"Let's go."

We get into the van and begin our climb up the hill and out of our development. We come to the first stoplight and wait with the other cars for the signal that it is okay to go. As we pull away, I look in my side mirror and watch my house, her car, my whole life shrink in the distance.

Leo doesn't turn the radio on, but still we are quiet most of the way. I wouldn't be able to hear him over my own thoughts anyway. At one point, he reaches over and takes my hand and rubs his thumb back and forth over the top of it to reassure me.

At first, I wish he hadn't done it, because it just made my heart leap toward him, and then I started to want all the other stuff again. But now I'm glad, because I think he is actually reassuring both of us, traveling together as we are, suddenly the same in a way, with just each other and our courage for company.

We pull into the bus station and Leo gets out of the van and walks me inside the terminal. He waits while I go up to the window and buy the ticket. I shove the change into my backpack.

"Is that all the money you have left?" I nod my head, and he hands me two twenty-dollar bills. "Here. Take this."

"No, Leo. Thank you, but—"

He shoves them into my pocket. "Take it."

I look away, my face all hot. "Thank you."

The announcer comes on and calls my bus: "Number 470 to Aberdeen. Boarding now. Bus 470 . . ."

"Well," I say, "I guess this is it."

"Are you sure you don't want me to take you?"

"I'm sure."

"Okay," he says.

"Leo? If I were older? Do you think you would like me? I mean . . . in *that* way?"

"Little girl, if you were older, you wouldn't give me the time of day."

I feel one tear overflow and fall down my cheek and into my mouth. "I'll look for you, Leo. In everything."

He smiles. "See ya round, kid." He turns to go.

"Leo?"

He turns back.

"Thank you."

"For what?"

"For being the only person on earth to notice my dimple."

He smiles at me, then takes my face in his hands.

"Smile," he says, so I do. He rubs his thumb gently over my left cheek and then he leans in and he kisses my dimple, lingering for just a moment at the corner of my mouth. We hover there, and I feel his breath on my face, his eyelashes on my cheek. Then he says, "Good-bye, Ellie. Be well. *Shine.*"

He hugs me again, and then I watch him walk away toward the van as I have seen him do so many times before. Only this time I am aware of all that he is taking with him, and all that he is leaving behind. Then I turn around and walk toward the bus, and all the days ahead.

sixteen

There is a four-year-old kid sitting in front of me on the bus. I know he is four because he held up his hand and pushed down his thumb to tell me he is "this many." His name is Thomas, and I made the huge mistake of wandering into the abyss of peek-a-boo as soon as the bus pulled away from the station. He popped his head up over his seat back a few times until I got the hint. Then I dutifully covered my eyes and said, "Peek-a-boo!" much to his squealing delight. I couldn't help myself; plus, my radar was down. Normally I would know to avoid this kind of thing, because once is never enough when you are four, and neither is two hundred and twenty. Finally I'd had it, and I flat out refused to play anymore. Thomas would pop his head up over the seat, his little face all lit up in expectation, only to meet my jaded stare. "Hi again, Thomas," I'd say, flat and monotone, my peek-a-boo voice long gone. He willfully tried to lull me back, but I stood my ground. Finally he said, "You no nice," and turned around in a huff. Now he is making faces at me between the seats.

I close my eyes for a while. I try to sort through all that has happened, but instead of the incessant chatter that is usually in my mind, it is quiet. There is a sense of motion, a sense of being. But my thoughts are unusually silent.

Occasionally, when I am not paying attention, there is a thought that comes along and tugs at my sleeve. Actually, it is more like a pull or a hunger than a thought. It is a sudden urge to get up off this bus and turn around, to go back home and fix this whole mess. *Maybe if I worked harder, I could make all of that right somehow.* But just as I am about to rise up from my seat and tell the driver I've made a big mistake, some other part of me takes over, pulls me back and says, *You stay right where you are.*

I guess that's the way it is when you finally see the truth. It's kind of like the Big Dipper. There was a time when I couldn't find it, ever. No matter how hard I tried, I just couldn't make sense of all those dots. I'd stare until I was dizzy, waiting for the pattern to emerge. I'd stare harder, expecting something *big*. Then, one day, there it was. Just sitting there, shining brightly among the other stars, its handle poised upward slightly, as if it were in motion, ready to shovel the whole sky. And now, I can't *not* see it. No matter where I am, if it is a clear night, all I have to do is look up and there it is, gently reminding me how blind I'd been.

I don't know what my dad's reaction will be. I rehearse my

lines in my head for when he is at the door. I try to imagine his face, but I have to stop doing that, because his face always looks sad in my mind, like he is worried the party is over. But if I really allow it, I picture other stuff too. Like, maybe when I get to my dad's, I'll ask him if he'd like to go see a movie. I saw an ad on TV for a new movie called *Dirty Dancing* that I thought looked good. And if he has a girlfriend and wants to bring her along, that will be okay. I won't care one bit. Maybe after the movie, if everyone's not too tired, we could go to the arcade next door to the theater and play some games. I remember my dad is really good at pinball. I could pick out some songs on the jukebox, and we could all get Cokes.

Thomas has stopped making faces at me. Instead, I can see him leaning on his mother's shoulder, fast asleep. Across the aisle there is a mother and daughter. The mother is chatting nervously; her daughter is pinch-faced and angry, you can tell, just waiting for her mother to do something to embarrass her. The daughter is wearing thick, black eye makeup, her hair is dyed a deep blue-black, and she is dressed in black from head to toe. She is one of those types who has her hand cocked and ready, metaphysically speaking, just waiting for anyone to give her one good reason.

I think about Gwen, the layers churning in her, masked so perfectly by her defiance, but all along keeping perfect rhythm. I know she is running hard and fast toward something that she hopes is better. But, in her desperation to get free of our mother, she has become just like her, learning the steps perfectly.

Victim and victimizer. Perpetrator and rescuer. Your turn, and now mine. And a one and a two and a . . . Who'd have known she could dance so well.

I'm afraid she will go back there, reenter the circle and try to get it right. I hope not. I hope that maybe someday she will be ready. Maybe someday she will come too. Until then, I know that she is the weight I carry, in me everywhere I go. I will be thirty years old, sitting on an airplane, and I will think how I should have bought two tickets, because she is right beside me anyway.

I think about Leo. I wonder what state he is in by now. Barely in West Virginia, I bet. He is probably flipping through all the radio stations, annoyed that it is mostly country music. I asked him to stop at Graceland when he went through Memphis, and he promised he would. I think about Priscilla and how all of that really turned out for her. You see, something I never told you is that *Elvis and Me* was actually a miniseries, and on night two, well, the whole relationship went pear-shaped. Sure, they got married and had a baby and everything, but Priscilla never really got her man. She spent the whole second night of the movie trying to get Elvis to pay attention to her. Finally, she got tired of it and started having an affair with her karate instructor.

I was mad at her for doing that, but now I think I understand it. With Elvis, she was the one who loved more, and she spent years chasing a phantom, trying to recapture what they'd once had. Then the karate guy came along and maybe she thought she loved him, but I think what she really loved was that he was the first person to come along and finally see *her*. And it kind of reminded her who she was, because after years of trying to get the attention of a remote and difficult person, she'd forgotten. And once she realized Elvis was never going to love her how she needed to be loved, well, she had to go carve out her own life and leave that dream behind.

I fluff up my backpack and lean against the window, watching the landscapes change out the window. Then I close my eyes and surrender to sleep.

The bus slows as we pull into the station. I grab my pack and do the hurry-up-and-wait thing as the passengers file out the door.

"Bye, Thomas," I say, but he sticks his tongue out at me and buries his face in his mother's shoulder. His mother's eyes apologize to me for his rudeness, but I smile and say, "It's okay. You're his safe place. That's a good thing."

I go straight to the line of taxicabs and jump into the first one. It smells like incense and body odor. My driver, Kashmir, asks me where I am going.

"Catonsville," I say. "331 Legget Street."

"That's pretty far."

I hold up Leo's two twenty-dollar bills. "This is all I have. Is it enough?"

Kashmir gives me a warm smile. "No," he says, "it isn't." My face falls, but he holds up his hand. "But it's okay. It's okay. You're just a kid. And you were honest. You did not wait until we get there. That is good."

Well, already things are looking up. I am on the right track after all. I bet my dad will have food in his house. All of my favorite things, like frozen pizza—the kind with a croissant for a crust—and Little Debbie snacks. Star Crunch is the best! Second only to Oatmeal Cream Pies and Keebler Fudge Sticks. Oh, *and* Utz potato chips! And probably tons of cereal, too, all different kinds so you can mix. And cold Diet Coke. Now I can have Celia for a sleepover! Oh, my gosh—maybe I can get a dog! Maybe *two*. I'd like two dogs with smooshy little faces who bicker between themselves in their little-dog language about whose turn it is to sit in my lap. But I will love them equally so I will be fair, and mostly I will love the sound they make when they stop at their bowls for a drink. I will put down whatever I am doing just to listen to it. It will be our conversation, them saying, *Thank you for remembering us,* and me saying, *You are so welcome.*

We turn onto my father's street, and I begin to gather my things. Kashmir slows to read the numbers on the mailboxes. There, ahead—the black mailbox. ROMA, it says. We pull up to his house. It is a small, white house with siding, nothing special. I don't see his car, just a motorcycle in the middle of repair. The flower boxes are empty, but they are there, ready.

I give Kashmir the forty dollars and head for the front door. The porch light isn't on and inside the house is dark. I go to the door and knock, but there is no answer. Kashmir pulls away and disappears down the street. I knock again. No answer. I try the knob, but it's locked. There is nobody here.

I stand with my head against the door frame, feel the ache swelling inside me. I don't know why I allowed this, the idea that things could be different for me. Of *course*. Of course he's not home. It is such a cruel thing to have hope. Hope just allows the fantasy until reality does its hundred-mile-an-hour hit-and-run. Then you just sit there, flattened and mortified by all your stupid hope. My mother was right. I bet he is out doing something single men do. Like getting his ear pierced.

What I don't understand is this whole big, mean, stingy world and why there's never any room for me in it. And if this is all I have to look forward to, just a world full of locked doors and people who won't let me in, then I don't want to live. I can't live in a world like that. I can't do it. I'm too tired. I look out at the darkened yard. There are no fireflies here.

I sit down on the concrete step and put my face in my hands, amazed by how many tears I have in me. My God, what am I going to do? I can't go back there. Even if I wanted to, I couldn't. And I don't know where I am all the way out here; I don't know where anything *is*. I don't know what to do. I can't do this. I'm so tired. And I'm *scared*. God, *some*body, help me. This is too much, I think. I am going to break. Why doesn't anyone want me? Someone help me. *Please.*

I pull my knees into me and begin to rock myself back and forth. I'm crying so hard I can't breathe. I reach for my backpack to get something to wipe my face on. And then I see the headlights. The silver two-seater. He's here.

I stand as my dad cuts off the engine and gets out of the car. He has bags with him, and he fumbles with the keys for a moment. Then he squints, seeing my figure in the dark.

"Hello?" he says. I am quiet, forgetting to breathe. "Who's

there?" he says, his voice rising. I take a step forward, into the light of his high beams.

"Hi, Daddy," I say.

I see it register on his face. "Ellie?" He drops the bags and rushes over to me. He searches my face like he's making sure it's me. "What are you doing here?"

My eyes start to fill. "I'm not ready to talk about it."

He nods his head, understanding. "Okay."

He puts his arms around me, and he squeezes so hard my feet lift off the ground. He pulls away, checking me again. I can see the tears, they are flowing down into his moustache. He shakes his head. "You little bugger," he says. "Come in."

He goes back for the bags and I pick up my backpack and we go inside the house. There is so much to say. And yet.

He offers me food but there is only beef jerky. "I'll go to the store tomorrow," he says. Then, "You look exhausted."

"I am."

He leads me through the house and into a bedroom, which he is using as a home gym. There are free weights and benches strewn around the room. I stumble over a dumbbell as I make my way to the bed.

I crawl under the covers and he sits down next to me.

"We'll talk in the morning, okay?"

"Okay," I say.

"Good night."

He walks over to turn off the light, then he stops, remembering. "Oh," he says, walking back toward me. "I want you to have this."

He reaches into his pocket and retrieves something and places it on the nightstand. I look over, and on the nightstand, next to an old conch-shell ashtray . . . is a key.

"Ellie," he says, "welcome home."

acknowledgments

First, I'd like to say thank you to God, the Universe, serendipity, and the thousands of unseen hands who all helped to create the words on these pages. Also, extra-special, warm-fuzzy thank you's to the following people:

To my daddy, Tony Paul, who always said I should "do something with my writing" (at which point I would roll my eyes and say, *Daaaad!*) and to my stepmom, Becky Paul: Thank you for so many things; but mostly the simplest thing—your constant love and availability. Thank you for creating a new normal, a foundation for me to jump from and return to. I love you both.

To Brian: You taught me that having a good idea isn't enough, and I would never have finished this book were it not for you. Thank you for all of your encouragement and support, for everything we were and everything we almost were. I love you. Still, and always.

To Kristen (my sister from another Mr., the Ethel to my Lucy): thank you for believing in me, for crying at the first draft, for the best twenty years any BFF could ask for. I don't know who or where I'd be without you.

To the "301 posse"—Laura, Hedy, Cynthie (and you too, Huffy!): You girls are my *map*. My love and loyalty are boundless and unending to each of you. I hope you will recognize yourselves in this story and smile. My thanks also to the entire Hayden, Huff, Quarles, and Apteker families.

To the wise and gifted Joyce Nelson Patenaude: Thank you for being such a great friend and mentor, and for helping me find the road back to myself.

Thank you to my agent, Diane Bartoli, and my editor, Julia Richardson, for being such smart awesome women, and for quite literally making my dreams come true.

To my first cheerleaders: Ross Fineman, Enio Rigolin, and Donna Larsen. Thank you for your time and your guidance and for believing in Ellie so much I just couldn't give up.

Thank you to the Maryland I remember. To fireflies and wanting more. To RR and everything after.

And my thanks especially to you, Mommy, for showing me how strong I am.